Istina and the Apostate

ISTINA AND THE APOSTATE

Religion, Genetics, and the Search for Meaning

Greg Olmsted

Dirty Business Publishing
Washington, DC

Library of Congress Control Number: 2018905311

ISBN 978-0-9861089-7-6 (trade paperback)
ISBN 978-0-9861089-6-9 (Ebook)

FIRST EDITION

Cover design by Kostis Pavlou

For all persons who seek the truth.

Contents

ALSO BY GREG OLMSTED

STRONG CURRENT TRILOGY

Under Water

Under Ground

Under Threat

OTHER NOVELS

Maritauqua Island (We Will Come Awake)

"*In this modern world,*
you need to know biology to be a good citizen."
MRS. EYLES, HIGH SCHOOL BIOLOGY
TEACHER

"*Love is the only sane and satisfactory answer*
to the problem of human existence."
ERIC FROMM

"If you see science being ignored or compromised,
speak up.
Think about where to raise your voice and then do it."
SARAH MARGARET "SALLY" JEWELL
UNITED STATES SECRETARY OF THE INTERIOR

1

I see her for the first time. She is wearing a cheerful magenta-colored leather coat, thigh length. Obviously Italian handcrafted. Her black, wavy hair is like a heavy shawl draped over her head and shoulders and coat. Thick black eyebrows, straight and slanting slightly upwards. Glossy red lips. A strong nose. Dark eyes staring down on her male companion, one step down on the down escalator.

I see her hand reaching out to touch his forearm. He turns around on the escalator, looking up at her. She rests her hand on his, his arm on the dirty black escalator rail.

I see them talking, smiling, laughing. They seem like a well-matched couple, his features like hers. He has a closely trimmed black beard. Otherwise, they are gender-opposite reflections of each other.

Two escalators going down. Two going up. The attractive couple on the escalator next to me, also going down into the metro station.

Three men in suits approach our down escalators. Are they perplexed like me, trying to figure out the Rome metro system? Like me, confused by the Italian signs? Another second and they will realize their mistake. Suppressing a smile, I wait for them to collide with the couple.

The woman yells "Run!" Her companion glances over his shoulder, sees the three men, and bolts up the escalator. As he passes on the side of the woman he grasps her hand, whips her around, jerks her up two escalator steps.

One of the businessmen rushes forward. He grabs the woman by her other arm and yanks her free, pulling her down the descending steps and off the end of the escalator. He slams her to the ground.

The second businessman jumps over her body—no, steps on and then over her body—and races up the down escalator after her escort. He yelled something that sounded like "Sin van un teeth!"

The woman tries to get up but the first businessman kicks her in the ribs twice. She collapses.

When I see the knife in his hand, the distance between us disappears. I grab his hand and force him to bury the knife in his own body, in his chest. It happens this fast—no thinking, just my body in motion.

The third businessman backs off, makes a "What the fuck?" face, yells an apparent obscenity at me, and then races up the up escalator.

I am left alone on the platform with the woman and the businessman, whom I stabbed in the chest. The woman and I make eye contact. My face asks, "What the shit?" I pull her gently to her feet.

"Help my brother! Please! Please help my brother!"

Again, no thinking, just my body in motion. I race up the up escalator. Reaching the top, looking around, I discover they are gone: the woman's brother and the two men in suits are gone, disappeared.

I race down the down escalator. Only the businessman is waiting for me, the knife still in his chest. The woman has vanished. A train has come and gone, and she has vanished.

No pulse from the neck. I leave him for dead and take the first metro to wherever the fuck it's going.

And then I take a train to Florence.

2

I hadn't eaten since I killed the man, but I had lost my appetite. My brain was blank, my body was numb, but I sat down for brunch. Once the food arrived, and I took the first bite of salad, I was ravenous. While I ate, my mind lost itself in the meal in front of me.

I remember pulling the tail off the shrimp, tasting the small pink-and-white body. It was delicious, lots of garlic and salt and butter. I had learned recently that Italians call their shrimp 'gambia.' Their rice, which the menu called 'risotto,' was mushy and not to my taste whatsoever. Italians ruin perfectly good rice. They make it creamy and then add weird stuff, like asparagus. In Hawaii we know how to prepare rice properly. Hawaiians make it fried and then add Portuguese sausage and yellow egg and small bits of orange carrot. Colorful and tasty, not mushy.

I once offended a waitress in Rome who asked me how my meal was. I had ordered risotto with butter beans, tomato and basil. I replied, "The rice is mushy and creamy. Someone doesn't know how to cook rice."

"Don't be ignorant," she scolded.

That hurt. Up until then, my only experience with food was grilling burgers and steaks after school during a part-time job at the Steak House. I knew nothing about the culinary arts, and definitely nothing about Italian cuisine. In fact, I knew nothing about any of the arts.

But I was not ignorant. I knew that I had upset the waitress – insulted her culture – so I apologized. From that moment on I decided to do things the Italian way: I rounded up the bill and left her a few coins. Later I spent my usual twenty percent American tip on a double gelato. I was in a new environment and it paid to adapt.

Last night I arrived in Florence. I had booked a short rental, a holiday Airbnb, but I hadn't slept well. The intense adrenaline rush had worn off, but I was still worried. I didn't know if the two surviving men—or others—were looking for me. Would the police suddenly show up? I just didn't know.

Now seated at the restaurant table, I studied a tourist map of Florence. My brain normally works well with topographical information. Not so well with chemistry and physics and other subjects. I do like geography and biology, though. I often dream of faraway places and adventures and that often involves studying maps, both paper and digital. Consequently I'm good at reading maps. But this map was hard to read. Or perhaps I just couldn't focus.

I noticed, though, that the Arno River cuts through Florence, in an area of the old city, an area the map labeled "historical city." I admonished myself. I needed to get to high ground, a vantage point, so I could study my surroundings. In the meantime, I studied the streets and piazzas of Florence in Google Earth.

Then I thought about the violence. I replayed the memory: three men in business suits attacking a handsome, middle-aged couple. The knife entering the businessman's chest. Everyone disappearing. I checked for a pulse. I learned that I had killed him. Numb with shock, I fled from Rome to Florence.

And then I thought about my Airbnb that I had reserved on the train ride from Rome to Florence. The one bedroom rental was not as safe as I had hoped. There were too many dark spots inside and outside the building, including a blind area in the stairwell just outside my room. And I did not see any closed circuit television systems to ward off intruders. Furthermore, there had been no one at the front desk in the reception area when I left for brunch this morning. But worst of all, I could open the exterior doors after hours without a key or access card or passcode, and just walk into the building. I would have chosen a safer Airbnb if I had not been dazed by the attack.

I studied the map and noticed the intersection of streets at the Piazza Carlo. The piazza and roundabout provided many alternate escape routes; at least eight streets came together in or near there. I decided to move to that area, to the "historical city."

I asked Aletheia, my personal scholar app on my iPhone, for help finding better lodging. With her assistance, I booked a suite at Al Palazzo Del Marchese Di Camugliano. It was located in the heart of Via del Moro and close to the Piazza Carlo. I liked that. It was a small, ten-room hotel and it included fitness facilities. I looked forward to working out. Too much stress that morning.

It was expensive, though. Very expensive. It wasn't the kind of place I could afford, so I placed it on my great-aunt's credit card. She was paying for my European education, a year-long, or possibly longer, trip around Europe.

No way I could afford my trip or the Airbnb, and especially an expensive hotel, a grand old palazzo. I just graduated from high school in Las Vegas. My father gambles. My mother is a maid for a local motel. They are divorced. Both are alcoholics.

I used to live with my mother in a disgusting trailer park outside Las Vegas, but I escaped. Actually, two loving people rescued me: my Uncle Keahi and my great-aunt. Now I'm on my way, I'm on an adventure—I just never imagined I'd kill someone. But what other option did I have? It was his knife. He was going to stab the woman, maybe kill her. I believe in the Golden Rule: help those in need, don't harm others. So I stopped him. But then he turned on me, so it became kill or be killed. That's an easy problem to solve. So I stopped him again. I sheathed his knife in his own body. It was the right action. I would do it again without hesitating.

I noticed a man at the next table gazing intently at me. Was something wrong? I started to feel uneasy. Someone else entered and he gazed at me, too, intently. Was there a mark of Cain? Or was this an Italian mannerism?

I had killed the man in self-defense, and probably saved the woman's life, too. But I still hadn't processed that emotionally. It happened so quickly!

I watched a man and woman meet at another table. I could see a greeting kiss. An air kiss. They sat close and touched arms lightly. Their gazes were intense. The woman wore knee-high boots, tall and sexy. I recognized the bold Fendi monster motif on her backpack: two large triangular eyes set against a black background. I had seen the Fendi backpack frequently in Rome, and I had asked Aletheia to identify it for me.

I studied the map again, strategically. I recalled what my

great-aunt had told me about Florence: it's a city of great ideas, brilliant artists. She called it an old "genius cluster." I had to ask Aletheia to define genius cluster for me. I think the world could use a new genius cluster. Yes, my home country of the United States, especially.

What would I do without Aletheia? I don't know. She was a graduation gift from my high school biology teacher, Mrs. Eyles. She is an expensive software program that integrates with my iPhone's Siri. I nicknamed her Aletheia. Aletheia has become my travel assistant. She helps me navigate through life's bullshit.

I wish I had bought stock in Aletheia's parent company when it went public! My biology teacher did. It is the biggest thing since Facebook. Even bigger.

Before I began my travels, while I was still in high school, I activated several of Aletheia's modules. Science is one of my weaknesses, even though I like biology, so I rely heavily on the science module. When I ask Aletheia a question, if the answers that she provides are scientifically correct, then she includes a green flag, based on scientific consensus or mathematics. If they are scientifically incorrect, then a red flag.

The tricky modules are politics, social issues, and history. Mrs. Eyles called them the "soft sciences." Her passion, like mine, was the natural sciences. When Aletheia answers a soft science question, she adds a banner across the top of the answer that ranges from yellow to red. Yellow means fact-checked, good URL sources, and probably accurate. Red means fact-checked and false, not true, a lie, bogus, nose-snot. A color between yellow and red is qualified with a note at the end of the answer, or a chyron if it is a video. When I ask political, social, or historical questions, I always check the color of the banner first. Then I read the footnote or chyron. And only then do I read the answer.

Since I'm not the smartest bodybuilder on the planet, I rely heavily on my Aletheia. When Mrs. Eyles gave me the gift she said, "This is not a shield from the world, but I hope that it will help you find your way." She added: "The challenge is to stay open to new things and new ideas."

Again I felt I was being watched, this time by a man with well-groomed hair and a business suit.

I tried to relax. I focused on my body and what I was feeling. My god! I had killed a man. I took my phone out of my pocket. My hand shook.

"Aletheia?"

'What can I help you with' appeared on the screen. After a moment she said, "Yes, Liko?"

I took a deep breath and set the phone on the table in front of me. I stared at it. "Aletheia, open your 'about' page."

The page opened. I focused on the screen and stared at the brightly colored Xeno Security logo. Xeno Security is the company that designed Aletheia. The logo appears in the top third of the screen, like a tattoo. I smiled. Aletheia's tattoo. Like, right on her forehead!

I took another deep breath and exhaled slowly.

The Department of Homeland Security had contracted Xeno Security to develop Aletheia's parent software. The program was a response to Russian military interference during the Clinton-Trump election. Homeland Security wanted a software program that could fact-check information available on the Internet.

Another deep breath . . . . my heartbeat began to slow.

A philanthropic foundation had funded an app for students based on Aletheia's parent software. They named it Xeno Assist Scholar. Mrs. Eyles, along with other high school teachers in the Las Vegas School District, beta-tested Xeno Assist Scholar during my senior year. She was impressed.

My breath expelled slowly . . .

Mrs. Eyles gifted me the app, surreptitiously, when I graduated. The app was meant for another science teacher, but he was diagnosed with Hodgkin Lymphoma, an aggressive cancer. Most unfortunate for the teacher, but lucky for me.

I wasn't a good student—more of a swimmer and body-builder—but Mrs. Eyles liked me. Maybe because she knew that I am passionate about marine biology.

A third of my schoolmates failed to graduate. Some can't even read. A few got low-skill, low-wage jobs. Others hustle tourists in Las Vegas. Almost all are alcoholics and gamblers. I know that several abuse their partners. Most should be in jail, but there aren't enough beds in Nevada.

I ran after I killed the man because I'd learned to run on the streets in Las Vegas. I never hurt anyone there, just juvenile stuff. Sometimes my coworkers at the Steak House and I would go to the strip after work. It's a twenty-four hour liquor town. But I believe in the Golden Rule now. After I joined the swim team at school and started lifting weights, my life changed. I stopped going downtown.

Finally my breathing normalized and my heart rate settled.

"Thank you, Aletheia."

"You are welcome, Liko."

I clicked her off.

Without Aletheia, I would be at the mercy of my emotions. Mrs. Eyles warned me about that. She said our first response to new information is always emotional. Those emotions are subconsciously paired with memories and images and such things. Mrs. Eyles said this response determines what I accept as accurate or inaccurate, true or false, truth or lie. She cautioned me that it has something to do with my fight-or-flight instinct.

Before brunch I had asked Aletheia for information about the police. According to Aletheia, the police had machine guns. I had seen that in Rome myself. Aletheia told me to call 112 for emergency help, 113 for police, 118 for first aid. She said all crimes should be reported to the nearest *commissarito di pubblica sicurezza*. She told me I could initiate a complaint: dead body in metro station in Rome. But she said it was mandatory to complete the *denuncia* at the station. Show up in person. I told her, "It isn't happening, oh wise one."

Nevertheless Aletheia had me on the lookout for *carabinieri* in dark blue uniforms with red stripes down the side and white shoulder belts; *Polizia di Stato* in light blue trousers with thin purple stripes and dark blue jackets; local police in white helmets, dressed in either black or blue, depending on the season—and since this was fall, they would be dressed in blue; and the *Guardia di Finanza* in gray and green uniforms with yellow flame insignia on their shoulders. I thought about these smartly dressed police and decided that they would be very impressive in a parade, but I had no desire to meet them.

I wondered why three businessmen in well-tailored suits would attack such a nice couple? After all, according to Aletheia, I was safer in Italy than in the US. The US has five times the murder rate and seven times the violent crime. Yet Italy has only half the police officers.

Was the attack related to drugs? Possibly. Aletheia said

more people in Italy used cannabis and opiates than the US. And Italy was the gateway for Latin American cocaine and Asian heroin to enter Europe.

So, if the attack was related to drugs, what were the businessmen's motives? They did not appear to be under the influence of drugs. They were too well-dressed to be short of cash. Perhaps I had stumbled into a turf war over the transportation and sale of drugs. Or maybe the three businessmen were good guys, arresting the couple, seizing drugs or money, a botched operation that resulted in a violent confrontation. Not likely, especially since one pulled a knife and was going to stab the woman. Besides, none of them were wearing those colorful uniforms, right?

There was clearly another possibility. The mafia. So on my way from Rome to Florence, Aletheia and I researched a possible Mafia connection to the assault. What I found did not bode well for me. That's why I moved to safer lodging later that day.

Maybe the three businessmen were members of an organized crime syndicate: either the Cosa Nostra or the 'Ndrangheta mafia. Probably the 'Ndrangheta. Aletheia told me the 'Ndrangheta had been kidnapping folks in Rome since the 60s and 70s. That's how they made their seed money to invest in cocaine, and then after 9/11 and the global recession, to invest in failing businesses and real estate. Today, according to Aletheia, "the 'Ndrangheta are more than 100 families, maybe 10,000 members, who steal 60 billion Euros per year from the global economy. They profit from narcotics, extortion, money laundering, and kidnapping."

What I prevented may have been an attempted abduction or kidnapping.

What if I killed a member of an 'Ndrangheta clan! Not

a good thing. Aletheia told me membership was based on blood relationships. These were family clans, sons following in fathers' footsteps. Uncles and nephews and aunts and nieces, all blood relatives.

This indeed was terrible news. There is no place in the world to hide from the 'Ndrangheta, unless you are in a witness protection program. And since I did the killing, and I fled the scene, I doubted a witness protection program would welcome me.

The Internet showed the 'Ndrangheta successfully took refuge not only in Australia and Japan, but also New York. Their homeland was Calabria, the toe boot of Italy, and the rugged Aspromonte mountains. If they came after me, that is where I would seek refuge. I would take the offensive and take the fight to them. But that was nervous bravado on my part. I was not thinking clearly. Right after killing a man I was confused.

I took a deep breath. I hoped it would clear the fog from my head.

I recalled they had an accent that didn't sound Italian. It wasn't Australian or Japanese. It was like German, but different. It was all confusing.

The Internet said the 'Ndrangheta are like an octopus with many tentacles, or a medusa with many venomous snakes. I imagined I could follow in the footsteps of Perseus and cut off the head of Medusa. I love those old Greek myths. But my thoughts were confused. I was not thinking clearly.

In the meantime, I decided not to trust anyone in a business suit.

3

I relaxed in the third floor windowsill of my room at the Al Palazzo Del Marchese Di Camugliano, overlooking Via del Moro. I had awakened earlier in the morning, feeling independent and wealthy, thanks to my great-aunt's credit card. My bedroom was impressive, but now I felt lonely. Independent and wealthy, but lonely.

I watched people walking to work. The local men were well-dressed, in simple, functional work clothes. The women were elegant.

I again resolved to thank my great-aunt for the opportunity. Until the tragic event in Rome, I had enjoyed my travels through Europe. I was still determined to take full advantage. I would not waste such a golden opportunity. The night before, after working out in the hotel fitness center, I had decided to stay in Florence for a week and then to leave Italy quietly. Like a mouse.

I smiled when I thought of myself sneaking out of the country "like a mouse" because I am 6 foot 3 inches tall and weigh 250 pounds. I used to be overweight and pudgy, but now I have the pecs and shoulders and waist of a competitive swimmer, and the powerful legs of a committed weightlifter. Two summers in Hawaii, visiting my Uncle Keahi and feeling embarrassed on the beaches, had convinced me to lose the baby fat.

And then I saw the magenta leather coat coming down the street. Unbelievable! She walked right beneath my window and continued towards the intersection of Piazza Carlo Goldoni. I couldn't believe it! Stunned, I mumbled Bogart's famous line: "Of all the gin joints, in all the towns, in all the world, she walks into mine."

I ran down the stairs and out the front door of the hotel. I crossed the *porte-cochère* and passed through the hotel gates and entrance that obstructed my view of the street. I surveyed the sidewalk . . . where was she? Where had she gone? I ran down the street to the piazza.

I reached the Piazza Carlo Goldoni and she was gone. All I could see were bicycles and mopeds neatly lining the left side of the street and a bright green cross—maybe a pharmacy sign? I was not sure—about a block away on the right side. And then I saw the magenta coat, one, one-and-a-half blocks ahead. I followed her, racing down the sidewalk along Borgo Ognissanti.

At the next intersection I jogged to the taxi stand in the middle of the Piazza Ognissanti. The piazza opened to the Arno River. Did she enter the six-story Westin Excelsior Hotel? The small, two-story church across the street? Or one of the other buildings fronting the piazza?

I saw a man holding a sign with a circle-backslash symbol negating the words "BIO-TEK." He was obviously a protester. As he turned around I read the back of his black T-shirt: SMETTERE DI OGM, in large yellow letters.

I quickly scanned the piazza for local police. I saw no white helmets, no blue uniforms, and no police vehicles.

And then I saw her talking to a woman outside an Italianate looking building, a tan-colored five-story façade with five large windows on each floor, and a flat tiled roof. The length of the building fronted the Arno River. She walked through the entrance ... and I followed her.

It was a funny feeling to enter a grand hotel—a former palace—because I didn't have a room and I was not an invited guest. I felt conspicuous. I passed through a plush reading lobby with large, brown, leather couches and high back leather chairs resting on expensive rugs on dark wooden floors. Reading lights were strategically placed, some outlined in crimson shades. I then came to the concierge area with two ornate secretary tables, each staffed by two or more women. The room was ornate, with glass chandeliers, a fireplace with a large mirror framed in gold resting on the mantel, and gold wood- or plaster-work on the walls. Everything was obviously expensive. After that I came to another spacious area with a huge crystal chandelier, a large white marble fireplace and a shiny white marble floor. I had never been in such an elegant hotel. I approached the half-circular wooden registration desk and three men nodded to me.

I ignored them, hoping that they would ignore me, and I walked up a flight of stairs. I thought the woman had probably taken the elevator, but I didn't know where the elevators were, yet. Halfway up the stairs was a stained glass window, with a larger-than-life-sized image of a servant girl in a brown dress, and an image of the hotel in front of her body, and a ribbon in her hands that read "Grand Hotel." Behind the servant girl was the dome of a church and a campanile-like tower, no doubt Florence landmarks I hadn't yet seen.

I stopped on the second floor and found myself in front

of a restaurant. I read the sign: "St. Regis Florence, breakfast, at the balcony of the Winter Garden."

The waiter seated me at a table on the balcony that wrapped around what must have been the Winter Garden restaurant below. A beige chandelier, preposterously ornate, hung in front of me in the center of everything. White tablecloths covered the tables.

And then I saw her again. She was at a table below me. I watched her spread jam on a croissant, take a bite, and set it aside to pick up a book. I deciphered the word "GENETICS" in large bold letters but everything else on the cover was in smaller print.

I watched men and women visit her table on their way to the buffet. They smiled, said a few words, laughed, and departed. She was popular. Perhaps she was attending a conference. She sipped a cappuccino.

I know nothing about genetics, other than I'm unhappy about the genes I've inherited. I call them the "Koholua genes," after my mother's side of the family. I inherited her big bones and big body. I used to weigh 305 pounds. When I was a kid, I thought we were monsters.

Thinking about genetics, I recalled my high school biology teacher, Mrs. Eyles. She was one of the few mentors in my life. I looked forward to her class three times a week, Monday, Wednesday and Fridays. There was never enough time to study any topic in detail, but I remember a class discussion on Watson and Crick, the co-discoverers of the molecular structure of DNA—the double helix, the blueprint of life. I also remember how surprised I was that it took only 50 years from the time of their discovery for other scientists to decode the human genome and to read it, end-to-end, identifying all the base pairs. That was not so long ago. Scientists are starting now to actually manipulate our genes. Mrs. Eyles called it genetic engineering.

Following the magenta woman's example, I also ate light, expecting that she might leave at any moment. I ordered a brioche liscia, juice, omelet, and cappuccino. I avoided the buffet. It was downstairs and I did not want the woman to see me.

Her thick black hair was impressive, and reminded me of my mother's and my Uncle Keahi's hair. They both have thick black hair. I do too. My mother's hair is like pahoehoe lava, flowing like ropes. My uncle's hair is thick and wavy, yet soft.

She finished her breakfast and pushed her chair back from the table.

After she left, I ferreted out information about the conference that she must be attending. I discovered a registration table strewn with conference materials just outside a large ballroom. What was the schedule? When and where could I see her again? The three-day conference was called Genetic Revolution: The Way Forward. The brochure stated that more than 300 scientists, legal experts, and ethicists were convening for a week in Florence.

I wondered, did the attempted kidnapping—that's what I had decided to call it, an attempted kidnapping—have something to do with this conference? With genetics? Genetic research? If so, what were the woman and these people involved in?

I glanced at the list of topics in the five concurrent sessions. The challenge session looked frightening: 'Mosaic embryos: off-target effects.' A topic in the ethics session also caught my attention: 'Altering human embryos – Chinese research.' And a long list of medical advances was impressive: lifelong protection against infection; mosquito breakthroughs – synthetic artemisinin and gene drives; xenotransplantation – pig hearts, baboons, and man. Geneticists were tackling childhood infections, malaria, and transplant rejection.

Frightening, impressive, and cutting edge – the topics intrigued me.

I read the biographies of the presenters. Was the woman a presenter? What was her name? If only the bios included pictures.

I scanned the list of conference sponsors. The conference was co-sponsored by pharmaceutical companies. One in particular had a catchy name: Xeno R&D. Did the attack have something to do with the biosafety of new drugs? Or biosecurity? I understood why the sign-carrying protester was outside.

Aletheia suggested a *Constant Gardener* theme, and even provided me a useful le Carré quote: "No drug company does something for nothing." So I added "evil multinational company" and "corporate greed" to my list of possible reasons a man died in a Rome metro station two days ago. Money and power versus human life and human rights.

So was the woman a GMO activist? Was she investigating unethical genetic research to expose it?

My heart jumped a beat. I imagined the woman raped and murdered like the woman in the movie *The Constant Gardener*. And I, like the woman's boyfriend, would die a lonely death. I scanned the restaurant but didn't see the men who had attacked her in Rome. Neither did I see any unsavory characters. Lots of business suits, though.

The conference program stated that an evening dinner was planned on Thursday, the day after tomorrow. Attendees were instructed to meet at 6:30pm at the St. Regis Hotel, with coach transfer to the Palazzo Capponi All'Annunziata.

It was a private event in a public setting. I could crash it. I could surprise the mystery woman. I could corner her, question her, and learn what had happened in Rome.

I decided to attend, so I would need a suit. A classic, navy blue, double-breasted, slim fitting (that's a joke) suit. With perfect fitting shoulders. There was a lot of money at the conference, I thought, so I needed a designer brand. Armani? Versace? Hugo Boss? Those were all the Italian brand names I knew.

I knew nothing about suits, and even less about Italian fashion. Later I learned that Hugo Boss was a German luxury fashion house, not Italian.

"It's too tight. It reminds me of a wetsuit."

The salesman stared at me as if I had just walked into his store with dog shit on my shoes. I hadn't meant to offend him, it's just that the suit he had me try on was uncomfortable. It fit terribly. Too tight in the chest and arms and neck. The upper arms were wrinkled and the sleeves looked twisted and tight. The jacket buttons strained as if they were about to pop off, and the fabric bunched into an X-shape on my chest. I did not want a suit that was going to squeeze me to death.

It reminded me of the ill-fitting, black neoprene wetsuit that I had forced my body into at the For Scuba Only quarry in Nevada. That was the disastrous quarry dive in which a girl drowned. She was only twenty-two. I was sixteen and anxious to pass my scuba skills test. I would have done anything that day to pass. Certification was my ticket out of the trailer park. My Uncle Keahi had promised to fly me to Waikiki, to join him for the summer, provided I got my certification. He wanted a dive partner. I wanted to escape.

I recall the young woman watching me put on my wetsuit. I was massive, soft, and undeveloped then, and it was an embarrassing moment. I forced my big feet through the narrow pant legs. I recall the black neoprene smelled of urine. When I stood up and tugged the pants over my chubby knees and bulky thighs and 46-inch waist, I could hardly breathe because of the ureic vapors. My stomach hung over the tight waistband. I was humiliated. I remember cursing my Koholua genes.

The wetsuit top didn't fit any better. I remember working my arms backwards into the heavy sleeves. I held my breath as I sucked in my massive stomach. And when I zipped up the top, starting from my left hip, crossing my chest and ending at my right shoulder, it was like sealing myself into a tight-fitting body bag. The memory still sends shivers down my back. When I straightened up, the top stretched and I had trouble breathing. I had to unzip the neoprene top halfway.

Everything has changed since then, though. I'm in excellent physical shape thanks to swimming and weight training and determination.

Well, my comment wasn't personal but the salesman bolted. I saw him coming back with an older, gray-haired man, impeccably dressed. I wished I had a suit like the older man. I had a feeling that I was about to be shown the front door.

"Sir, may I assist you?" His posture and haughty attitude reminded me of Mr. Bates on *Downton Abbey*, except this man was Italian, not English. I wondered if Italians have personal butlers, too? I had no idea. I'd ask Aletheia later.

"I need a suit."

He looked at what I was wearing and shook his head. "What is the occasion, sir? Work? Personal time?"

"I'm here on vacation, but I'm going to a formal dinner." I caught his eye and added, "I want to make a good impression. I'd like something Italian, or at least Italian made."

"All of our suits are made in Italy, sir. Exquisite craftsmanship."

I thought to myself, *Of course*. But I said, "Perhaps you could recommend one?"

"Let's get you out of this. It is much too small." He walked behind me and peeled the sport jacket off. It was so tight that the sleeves turned inside out as he tugged it off. If I were still that fat kid at the Nevada quarry, I'd be embarrassed. But now I was lean and cut.

"What would you recommend?"

He smiled. I had asked him twice now for his recommendation, and this seemed to please him. "Who is your favorite actor?" he asked, surprising me.

"Schwarzenegger."

"Then Canali, sir." He handed the jacket to the young man standing next to him, turning him instantly into an assistant. "I would recommend Canali. Arnold Schwarzenegger wore Canali in *True Lies*. Did you see *True Lies*, sir?"

"Yes. I've seen all of his movies, except for his latest." He should have quit at the top of his game. Yeah, I remembered him wearing a suit in that movie. He looked great. Pure action.

"I have a Canali suit that you will like."

"I would like something with flat-front trousers." I

thought pleated pants were for dandies. "I'd also like a jacket that is cut on both sides."

"Double-vented?"

"Yes. Double-vented." I thought that a single cut, or vent, over your butt crack was worse than pleated pants.

I followed him to a corner of the store and to a rack of suits. I guessed this was the Canali section.

He whipped out a tape measure and told me to stand straight and hold my arms at my sides. He took multiple measurements. Then he had me extend my arms to shoulder height. He again took measurements. "I recommend a two-button, fully lined jacket." He measured my neck and waist, too.

He sorted through several jackets and selected one. He took it off the hanger and helped me into it. "This is a classic Italian fit."

I felt the texture. "Is this wool?"

"Yes. It is wool."

"It's still too tight," I said.

He helped me try on another. It was dark gray. "It looks good." He grasped the top button of the jacket and pulled it away from my chest. "This one fits close to your body without being too snug."

Next he had me try on a pair of pants. His measurements must have been perfect because the waistband was snug but not tight. I was impressed.

I was soon standing in front of the store alterations expert, who was marking my new suit with white chalk.

The tailor seemed pleased with both the suit and the potential fit. "You need more drape for your arms," he said. He had me move my arms forward and then back to my sides. He made white hatch marks all over the back and sides and shoulders of my new suit. "Now, that should be good in the shoulders."

The tailor handed me back to the gray-haired salesman again. "Do you need shirts, belts, socks?" the salesman asked.

"Yes. All of those."

He deftly selected two shirts—a white one and a plain, pale blue one—and dark gray socks. We picked out a pink tie. Yes. Pink! But when he placed it next to the white shirt and gray jacket it was a good choice.

"I recommend a reversible belt. Black and brown. Black belt for black shoes. Brown belt for brown shoes."

I was being tutored like a complete novice, but I had asked for his recommendation. I permitted him to select a black leather calfskin belt.

Swallowing my pride, I said, "And shoes? What do you recommend?"

He took me to the shoe department, and with the assistance of another gray-haired man I soon had a new pair of black Italian leather shoes. Size 14EEE. My shoe size was in stock and, for the first time in my life, my big feet were not an embarrassment.

I was so pleased with his service that I made an unnecessary purchase: a stiff bristled clothes brush. He assured me it was essential to maintain the appearance of the jacket. "Dry clean seldom," he said. "Brush often."

I placed everything on my great-aunt's credit card. The salesman assured me that the suit would be altered and ready for pick up late afternoon tomorrow, in time for the dinner.

I left the luxury Italian clothing store having purchased a 100 percent wool Canali suit and accessories. I hoped I had made a good choice. As I passed a bookstore I entered on a whim to look for a bestseller or a science book about genetics, but everything was in Italian except for the travel book section. So I bought a tourist book on Florence in English.

What was I to do now? I went to a café and drank a coffee, perusing the tourist book.

I watched a woman flirt with a man. She smiled at him. I could not see his reaction because he was seated with his back to me. She gazed into his eyes, tilted her head to the side, and looked away. She giggled and then gazed at him again.

I mused about the woman in the magenta coat. She was obviously smart because she was attending the conference. She also looked tough, savvy. All business.

Maybe I should return to her hotel. See if I could find her. See what sessions she was attending this afternoon. Maybe I could find out something about her. Who was she talking to? Was she with anyone? A coworker? Was there someone staying with her at the hotel? A husband? Boyfriend? The man I'd seen her with in Rome, her brother, she'd said? She was middle-aged. Would she be interested in someone as young as me?

I could sneak into the conference. Why not? I was wasting my time with this touristy stuff.

As I perused the tourist book again, the word "mafia" jumped out at me. I followed it through the index to a description of an explosion at a place called the Vasari Corridor. Aletheia provided additional information, so I spent the next hour researching the tragic events that occurred 27 May 1993 when the mafia set off a powerful car bomb in a street behind the Uffizi Gallery, near the Vasari Corridor, here in Florence.

I decided to visit the site, not only because of the explosion but also because of the Vasari Corridor, a protected passageway. I found the idea of an elevated, protected passageway fascinating. Who builds something like that? And why?

So I asked Aletheia. The long story short: the Medici family, who made an enormous amount of money because they were the Popes' bankers, built the Vasari Corridor. For some reason, the Medici got a percentage of all the donations, rent, and taxes that the church collected, starting about 500 years ago. They also profited from selling indulgences, or buying one's way out of sin.

In addition to acquiring enormous wealth, the Medici titled themselves Dukes, replacing the Republic of Florence. No wonder they had enemies! They needed a way to safely travel between their administrative palace and their home palace, so they hired a man named Vasari to build them a defensible passageway—a corridor—from palace to palace. Five hundred years later, the corridor served as a museum, and when the Cosa Nostra set off that bomb in a white Fiat van, it destroyed paintings, including a Rubens. The explosion also killed a couple and their young children who had been renting an apartment on the third floor of a nearby medieval tower; it collapsed on them while they slept and they were found on the ground level, crushed. All of this received a green banner by Aletheia. All true.

I took a taxi to the site of the explosion and saw the olive tree that had been planted as a memorial. Aletheia translated a plaque in Italian for me: "This olive, this generous mythological symbol of holiness and great values, has the emblematic capacity to regenerate its productivity, although it suffers event due to nature or man." Nice. I wondered if it made any difference that olive trees grew wild in Calabria, the home of the 'Ndrangheta mafia? It was little condolence that the bosses and members of the clan responsible for the deaths of six people, including two children—one younger than one year of age, the other less than ten—and their parents, were sentenced to life imprisonment.

I returned to my room in the Al Palazzo Del Marchese Di Camugliano hotel. It was so comfortable and luxurious, I decided to stay inside and read my new tourist guide of Florence. Enthralled with the city, I got up to look out the window again, the window where I had been sitting when I saw the woman earlier in the morning. Suddenly an idea occurred to me. Could the attempted abduction have been related to terrorism? Maybe it had nothing to do with the mafia or pharmaceutical companies.

Excited, I fired off a series of questions and Aletheia replied, "Abu Omar case." So I spent the next two hours researching about a radical Egyptian cleric who had been in Italy on an asylum passport, but who was abducted by the US CIA as he walked to his mosque in Milan to pray. Damn! My research showed he was shoved into a van, driven to a US air base in Italy, flown to Germany, and then transferred to Cairo. The Egyptians had tortured him. After four years in an Egyptian prison he was released.

Aletheia found an article about the abduction on the Internet for me. An independent Italian prosecutor and an Italian judge convicted twenty-two CIA agents, a colonel in the US Air Force, and several Italian secret agents of kidnapping. If any of the Americans were caught traveling in Europe, they each faced five years in prison and a 1.5 million pounds fine, payable to Abu Omar and his wife. Astonishing!

The more I thought about that case, the more I wondered if the three men in business suits were working for the US CIA. Or perhaps the Italian Military Intelligence and Security Service. During the Bush-Cheney administration a series of US Department of Justice memoranda had authorized torture methods. Aletheia said the US CIA used those torture methods, including waterboarding, around the world.

I wondered: if there were US CIA operations back then, why not now? The US was still waging a global war on terrorism and, for all I know, still using extraordinary rendition, as they had done with Abu Omar. Were the woman and her companion targets of the CIA?

Sitting in my plush room, I wrote up my ever-growing list of suspects on the fancy hotel stationary: a drug gang, 'Ndrangheta mafia, Cosa Nostra mafia, one or more pharmaceutical companies, crazed activists, a jealous coworker, US CIA and/or the Italian SISMI. And then I wrote: *What was the motive? Money and power? Corporate greed? National security? Random violence? Jealousy?*

The bedroom clock on the nightstand displayed 11:35. I decided that I needed to be in bed before midnight. Tomorrow would be a big day. I had to pare down the list of suspects. I had to talk to the mystery woman.

I quickly brushed and flossed my teeth and washed my face with soap and water. When I climbed into the bed the sheets felt cool. I don't wear pajamas. I hate the things. Pajamas get all wrapped around you, especially if you toss and turn, which I imagined that I would. Why wrestle with unnecessary bedclothes?

4

The next morning I needed coffee desperately. When I woke up, the cotton sheets on my hotel bed were soaked with sweat, and I had sleep-clouded memories of combat with the 'Ndrangheta mafia. It had been more like a zombie war. A mafia version of *Night of the Living Dead*. The zombies were "made men" in business suits. One in particular stood out: he had no tie, a popped collar, and his shirt cuffs were turned back to reveal an expensive watch, probably Italian. Definitely a "made zombie:" good taste, manners, polish, and a certain elegance, but no soul. He wanted to eat my brain and then my heart. A real cannibal. I hunted him and his family in the hidden rooms and tunnels excavated beneath his home. Sadly, for every family I killed another sprang up. A real-world nightmare.

Outside, there were more protesters. I counted seven, mostly men. The protester from yesterday now had a bullhorn. He was leading a small group in a tight circle in the piazza directly across from the hotel. He chanted, "Say no to GMO," and they repeated "Dire di no, di OGM." It was kind of catchy: "Say no to GMO. Dire di no, di OGM. Say no to GMO. Dire di no, di OGM." And round and round they went. Irritating, though!

I saw a light blue vehicle parked nearby. The shaded windows were up but I could make out the shapes of two figures seated in the front seat. I couldn't see any details. I assumed they were local Florence police.

I walked directly up to the protesters and then at the last moment I detoured briskly around them, as if I they had inconvenienced me, a guest at the hotel. I walked confidently to the hotel entrance. I glanced back over my shoulder. The protesters and the police had taken no notice of me. I smiled at the hotel porter and walked confidently into the hotel.

Finally seated at a breakfast table on the balcony overlooking the Winter Garden, I spread salted butter and sweet marmalade on my croissant; I think I ordered what the woman had yesterday. I took a bite and sipped my cappuccino. It was steaming hot.

Then I saw her again. She was the only woman among three men seated at the table below me. One wore Armani, which I recognized now after my suit shopping adventure. Another was seated close and touched her arm as she spoke. He was wearing a red scarf wrapped around his neck. I could see the intense gazes of men all around her, including the nearby tables, or was it my imagination?

The woman was beautiful. Thick, voluptuous lips, turned outward and glossy. Thick black hair, now twisted into long braids. She had styled her hair differently. Large, hazel eyes.

Why had someone attacked her?

I had been looking forward to tonight's dinner but now I felt nervous. I told myself I didn't have to go. I could

return to my hotel, pack my travel kit, and quietly leave
Florence. Why not?

It was too early to pick up my suit so I ventured out to
il Grande Museo del Duomo. With Aletheia's help, I had
booked a special guided tour on-line that offered "extraordinary views of the city and Brunelleschi's Dome." I was
not interested in the dome or baptistery or bell tower, but
I wanted to see Florence from a high vantage point. The
tour, which let me skip the queues, also included a crypt.
I hoped the crypt would not be anticlimactic after last
night's zombie dreams.

I arrived early at the Piazza del Duomo and gathered my
bearings. In front of me, according to Aletheia, was a 1,500-
to 1,600-year-old baptistery. To my right was a 700-year-
old *campanile*, Giotto's Bell Tower, and also an old cathedral and dome. I wanted the view from the dome. I needed
the lay of the land: a strategic survey of Florence.

I noticed the baptistery building had an unusual shape. I
walked around it, counting its sides, expecting five like the
honeycomb of bees, but arrived at eight equal sides. How
did that come about? I wondered. It jogged something in
my memory, though. Yes, an eight-sided gazebo, the coronation pavilion on the grounds of the Iolani Palace, the
only royal palace in the United States. It was in my homeland of Hawaii. Of course it was no longer a coronation
pavilion. Today it was a bandstand.

I had spent many Friday afternoons there, seated on a
folding chair, enjoying the Royal Hawaiian Band, watching the girls eat plate lunches during their lunch breaks.
I enjoyed seeing pretty girls on the beach, too. I miss
Hawaii.

I now noticed the unusual exterior of the baptistery. The sides were colored marble, white with green inlay. Each of the eight corners boasted a zebra pattern of white and green vertical striping. Weird.

So this was the oldest building in the square? Its age was not exactly known so Aletheia gave me a range: 4th to the 7th century. I'm not good with history, but I could remember a few impressive dates. Sixteen hundred years is not that long ago, not really. The cretaceous Tertiary mass extinction occurred 65 million years ago, when a meteorite impact wiped out the dinosaurs. The Permian mass extinction was even older than that, 248 million years ago; that's when 96 percent of all species vanished. What other dates did I know? Not many. I knew that the US Civil War lasted four years, from 1861 to 1865. World War I, a terrible tragedy, lasted another four years, 1914 to 1918. And then there was World War II, a little longer at six years, 1939 to 1945. Uncle Keahi had taken me to the USS Arizona Memorial in Pearl Harbor during my first Hawaiian vacation. Then the Vietnam War, my father's war. And fortunately, I was too young for President Bush's war in Iraq, which evolved into The War on Terrorism. I guessed the baptistery was significant because it was built more than a thousand years ago, when men still believed the sun rotated around the earth.

I noticed a gaggle of nuns admiring the baptistery doors. I looked around but didn't see any priests or other obviously religious people. I wondered: what did the nuns see, what were they thinking, what did they believe? For myself, I saw a group of women dressed in traditional religious habits. I think nuns are as delusional as Don Quixote, believing the world to be exactly as they declared it to be, contrary to common sense. I believed that I would rather wake up in the morning as a . . . what?

I took my iPhone out of my pocket again. As I fumbled with the phone I thought maybe I should invest in an Apple watch? Or wireless ear buds with a microphone? I'd have easier, faster, smoother access to Aletheia. Convenience is everything.

"Aletheia, what is the first line of *The Metamorphosis?*"

"Liko, let me think about that. OK, I found this on the web for 'what is the first line of the metamorphosis': 'When Gregor Samsa woke up one morning from unsettling dreams, he found himself changed in bed into a monstrous vermin.'"

"Thank you, Aletheia."

"It is my pleasure."

What I found astonishing is that I woke up this morning, after tossing and turning all night long, unchanged. Yes, I was tired and hungry, but I had not metamorphosed. Physically, mentally, spiritually, I was still Liko. Yet I had killed a man three days ago and was still myself. Shouldn't I be different?

"Aletheia, has the world metamorphosed? Maybe that's what happened. Has the world metamorphosed?"

"OK, I found this on the web for 'has the world metamorphosed': "Climate change is the most pressing issue of our time. It is changing the political order of the world.""

"Aletheia, that's depressing. Thanks a lot."

"I aim to please."

Biding my time, I examined the three sets of bronze doors. I recognized creation stories from the Bible cast in bronze on the panels covering the doors. One Internet source described them as "desert tribal mythology expressed in bronze reliefs by artists in Florence."

I checked my phone. I still had thirty minutes before I could climb to the top of the cathedral.

I gazed at the panel that shows the beheading of John the Baptist. In bible school I had been told that he ate honey and locusts. I like honey. I eat it by the spoonful. But I've never eaten a locust, raw or roasted to a crisp. I Googled it. And then I read in Leviticus, the Jewish law, that it is okay to eat locust. Aletheia told me that the authors of Leviticus didn't know how many legs flying insects had! They said: Don't eat flying insects that have four legs, except for crickets and grasshoppers and locusts and katydids. But all insects have six legs! Three legs on one side, and three legs on the other. So I asked myself, could John the Baptist have eaten flying roaches? The answer according to Leviticus was clearly 'yes.' That's nasty.

Next I saw Christ on a panel with his glorious long hair. A Superstar in all his antique bronziness, in a relief made hundreds of years ago. I surmised that the sculptor, back in his day, wasn't familiar with the New Testament verse, "Does not even nature teach you that it is a shame for a man to have long hair?" Actually, I have to take exception to that verse. I know biology. Long hair is a matter of choice, not nature. The length of one's hair is a cultural thing. Biologically the length of your hair makes little difference if you are man or woman.

Maybe I will grow my hair out. At least a little longer, maybe as long as Uncle Keahi's hair. I keep my hair short because it is thick and wavy, and that makes it a challenge to manage. The idea of grooming my hair every day doesn't sound fun to me. Maybe the mystery woman does, but I don't. She must have gone to the hotel salon the previous evening. Uncle likes to style his hair, too. I think

Uncle Keahi would like her hair. I admit I think it is incredible. Her hair reminds me of strands of salt water licorice taffy. I love licorice. And I like taffy.

I gazed at another door and studied the left column, second puzzle from the top. I saw a bronze relief of a man lying on the ground, leaning on his right arm, under a barrel. He was naked, his cloak bunched up underneath him and barely covering his stomach. His left hand rested on his knee. His legs spread apart and his penis showed. His right hand was holding an empty bowl. The expression on his face was unhappy. His mouth was open. I could see animals: an elephant, a lion and lioness running, and an eight-point buck. I solved the puzzle: Noah was drunk and the animals were from his ark.

I looked again at Noah spread out on the ground naked. Why did he get drunk? Aletheia reported that the Bible didn't say. Was it because he was upset that all his relatives, friends, and neighbors drowned? He took only two of each kind of animal, so imagine how many herds of sheep, cattle, and camels drowned. Imagine finding all those drowned people and bloated animals after the water receded. I couldn't drown a litter of kittens. I was actually in that position one time and I refused to do it.

I remembered, though, getting blitzed at my Uncle Keahi's studio. I helped myself to a big bottle of red wine. A serious mistake. I lay on the floor watching the ceiling fan for a couple of hours, and when my uncle returned from work it was embarrassing. I had gotten drunk because I was embarrassed about being overweight, upset with my Hawaiian genes.

My mother gets drunk because she feels disrespected by my dad. She is a lonely alcoholic. My dad drinks because he enjoys being drunk, and he is a mean asshole when he drinks. My uncle drinks because he is unhappy, and paralyzed by indecision. He wants to dance, to chant, to perform but he is scared to leave the security of his low-paying government job. He behaves as if he has been caught in a strong current that has pulled him out to sea, away from everything he loves and desires. He is a sad case. Uncle sometimes drinks on his lanai until he passes out.

I don't want to be like my mother, father, or uncle. And I definitely don't want to be like Noah! I only drink when I am frustrated or disappointed.

It only took a few minutes to debunk the story about Noah and God's ark. That's really all the time it took, a few minutes. Simple math and common sense. First I calculated the size of the ark and the volume that it could carry. Second, I estimated the number of species on the earth and their volume. And then I compared the volume of the ark and the volume of the animals that God commanded Noah to load. Fortunately one doesn't have to know algebra, one must only understand math and reason. I must admit, though, Aletheia did the calculations.

I suppose the panels were well made, but I was not interested in the art. I was just killing time. My goal was to see Florence from a high vantage point, the top of the church dome. While I waited, I deciphered yet another puzzle. I saw a man on top of a mountain. Another man in the sky handed him two tablets. I suspected that the man in the sky represented God, but he wore a funny three-pointed hat, the kind kids make out of paper, and that looks like a sailboat. Two other long-haired men in the clouds blew long slender trumpets. I suspected they were angels because they had wings. I solved this panel, too: Moses receiving the Ten Commandments from God, the first of many religious laws.

I broke one of the commandments. I killed a man three days ago in the Rome metro. So, as far as keeping the Ten Commandments, I knew that I was one for ten. The guy was dead. Definitely dead.

I was curious, though, how was I doing on the other nine? I took out my phone and Googled the Ten Commandments. I almost laughed out loud because they popped up on my phone as pictures of two stone tablets. Standing before the bronze door I read the tablets.

The first four commandments were easy to disregard because they are all about God wanting people to worship him. I dislike that. Plus, I'm an atheist so those four don't apply to me anyway. I've been an atheist since the tenth grade. My epiphany occurred at the end of "Gimme Some Truth" while I was listening to John Lennon's album *Imagine*, lying on my bed at home in the trailer park. I suddenly wanted to know the truth about Christianity, so I spent the rest of the weekend on the Internet. I discovered a lack of evidence for the biblical stories and doctrines I had been taught. My loss of faith was quick: less than forty-eight hours. No struggle, just a hard look at the facts. Later that year I read the Bible cover to cover and that reinforced my disbelief.

As for the Fifth Commandment, "Honor thy mother and father," not a chance. My father does not deserve to be honored. Sadly, for some people, like me, that is a fact that just can't be whitewashed. My father is an alcoholic, a gambler, and abuses my mother and me. He doesn't deserve my respect and I definitely will not honor him. It makes no difference to me what a group of desert nomads said thousands of years ago. They didn't know my father.

I love my mother. During my senior year in high school I helped her move from her trailer to an apartment. I am the one who paid the first and last months' rent, including the utility deposit. I used my earnings from working at the Steak House. I am also the one who rented a truck and moved all her stuff. I had an ulterior motive: I didn't want to have any regrets about leaving her and starting out on my own. I wanted no guilt or self-reproach.

But back to the Sixth Commandment: I killed someone in self-defense while protecting someone else. I'd do it again without hesitating. Any sane person would. Any animal would defend itself, too. On this topic my mind is as untroubled as the sun rising in the morning. However I would like to know why he died. Why did he attack the woman? Some things need to be answered, and this was one of them.

I looked at my phone. I still had plenty of time before the special tour started. I had arrived way too early. Next time I would judge the distance on the map better.

Regarding the Seventh, Eighth and Ninth Commandments: I've never committed adultery or stolen anything, and I am honest. In fact, I am so honest it may be a weakness sometimes.

Thankfully I have Aletheia. With her help I make the best decisions I can—informed decisions, based on facts, evidence, and proof. And scientific consensus, too, whenever it is available. Sometimes it is humbling to admit that I think or believe something that is in the red, that is incorrect. But I get over it. I always get over it.

What irks me are people who lack common sense.

It was Mrs. Eyles who taught me about common sense, honesty and truth, and probably freedom of speech, too. And it all started, amazingly, in her high school biology class while we were talking about sex. We were all attentive because we were discussing the use of condoms to prevent unwanted pregnancies and sexual diseases. She provoked a lively discussion, and we learned a lot about birth control that day.

She had written on the board: "Should common sense trump moral teaching?" By the end of the class the question had been rephrased: "Should common sense trump fear-based moral teaching?" That's what the class decided was the real problem: not 'moral teaching' but 'fear-based moral teaching.'

That evening, between school and my job at the Steak House, I stopped by her house and we continued the discussion. I did that sometimes during my senior year. So did some of the other students. We stopped by to talk about whatever was happening in our lives, and shared problems we were having, and she was always a sounding board, listening to us.

"Liko, you were quiet during class today. What were you thinking?"

"About using condoms when the church says it's immoral."

"Yes." Her smile encouraged me. "And what do you think about that?"

"I don't know. People believe all kinds of things. Even crazy things. So what?"

"So what?" Her smile faltered. Mrs. Eyles did not tolerate mental laziness. "Two plus two equals four, Liko."

"What about imaginary numbers?" I thought I was being smart.

"Do you live in an imaginary universe?"

"Maybe."

Her face crumpled. She had no tolerance for outright nonsense, either.

"No. I don't." I self-corrected, suddenly ashamed of my childish answer.

"Alternate facts are not real facts. They're falsehoods."

The whole population of the United States of America had learned that lesson during the Trump administration. It had not been my personal lesson, though, until that evening in Mrs. Eyles' living room.

From that moment on, I committed myself to applying this new rule. I called it "Mrs. Eyles' Rule: Truth is easy." It was the best advice that I received from an adult. I am deeply indebted to her. I have since learned that truth is also hard. In response to President Trump's bashing of the American press, *The New York Times* newspaper took out a television ad during a Super Bowl game. The gist of the ad was: "The truth is hard. The truth is hard to find. The truth is hard to know. The truth is more important than ever." I liked that, too.

And the Tenth Commandment? I don't covet anyone's house, possessions, or wife. My great-aunt has a fantastic home at Black Point Beach, and I wouldn't mind living there after my travels. And it is nice having Auntie's credit card. But I don't covet anything.

My world travels are a no-strings-attached agreement between my great-aunt and me. Her sole condition is that I consider attending university after my adventure. She'll pay for my university too, she says.

"Aletheia, how much time before the tour starts?"

"Eleven minutes."

Damn! "Aletheia, set a reminder. Remind me when the tour starts."

"I've set an alarm for 1pm."

I had nothing to do but decipher one more puzzle: the bottom panel on the left side of one of the doors. It was too easy, though. It was the story of David slaying the giant Goliath. Everyone likes the story of an underdog! And children like stories about giants. Even me.

According to Genesis, before the flood, giants walked upon the earth. They were the Nephilim, and they were the offspring of the "sons of God" and the "daughters of men." I don't believe in Nephilim any more than I believe in hobbits, fairies, leprechauns, or Menehune.

One story about the giants was amusing. After the Israelites escaped from Egypt, Moses sent spies into their promised land to see what challenges lay ahead. After 40 days the spies returned and told Moses that they had seen giants. Moses and his followers believed the spies, that giants existed. They also believed that they could not conquer the giants, even with God's help. So God punished their lack of faith by making them wander in a desert for 40 years. The original *National Lampoon Vacation*? Were the Griswolds Jewish?

Even Hercules, the mythical Greek and Roman hero—who is also my mythical hero—performed better than Moses and the Israelites. Hercules helped Zeus defeat the mighty giants Porphyrion and Alkyoneus in a great battle for control of Olympus. Roman storytellers said the giants had dragon scales on their feet. They were frightful to look at, just like the giants in the Bible.

Waiting for the phone alarm to sound, I went back and looked at the Noah panel again. According to the Old Testament, God created the rainbow after Noah's flood: "I have set my rainbow in the clouds, and it will be the sign of the covenant between me and the earth." Really? In my eighth grade high school science class I learned that rainbows appear due to the nature of light, the refractive index of water, and the shape of raindrops. Rainbows existed billions of years before humans existed, so rainbows existed obviously billions of years before God's big flood.

I remembered seeing a beautiful double rainbow on the Big Island of Hawaii while I was hiking through Volcanoes National Park. I remember thinking at the time that if I could only walk fast enough, I could pass beneath the double rainbow, and then for a moment one rainbow would be in front of me and the other rainbow would be behind me. Now that would be cool! It was impossible, though, just as the timing of God's covenant was impossible. Just because it makes a good story doesn't make it true.

Similarly, it didn't make sense for God to create the plants before he created the sun. But that is what he did, according to the author of Genesis. It violates common sense. Who would plant marijuana before they set up plant grow lights?

I stepped into the baptistery, a giant step back in time. My feet crossed marble inlay. I walked over the signs of the zodiac, a pagan decoration! The merging of two beliefs, two religions?

I noticed two big stone boxes—sarcophagi—and looked at the wide, black geometric designs on the wall and small, black and white patterns on the floor. And then the interior of the dome popped, filled with golden mosaics, figures on a gold background. Another long-haired Jesus with people beneath his feet, his right hand directing believers to joy and his left hand dismissing nonbelievers to hell, where they would suffer forever and forever. His hands and feet showed the nail marks of his execution.

I bristled. At the end of my junior year, I had spent a few weeks studying the Bible. I had learned that hell and eternal suffering were pagan creations. There is no hell in the Old Testament. The word 'hell' in the Old Testament is a translation of Sheol, a Hebrew word. Nowhere in the Old Testament is Sheol a place of endless torment for violating the laws of Moses. In the Old Testament, rewards and punishments are received in the current life, not after death. God made the penalty for eating of the Tree of Knowledge of Good and Evil death, not a place of endless torment. The bad people in Sodom and Gomorrah were destroyed, but they were not sent to a place of everlasting fire and brimstone. Neither was anyone or any people in the Old Testament warned about eternal damnation for violating the laws of Moses. Yes, people were warned about destruction and punishment in the here and now, but never eternal damnation. Everlasting brimstone is a concept that the early Christians borrowed from the pagans. Now, standing in the cathedral, staring at the mosaics on the dome, I resolved to have Aletheia fact-check this later.

What kind of people imagined a gross being and called him Satan, imagined a place for him to rule called hell, and then imagined that all people who disagree with them will spend eternity with Satan, suffering in hell? To imagine such a terrible thing and then to wish it upon the world is truly what? Sadistic? Especially when you see how artists depict hell: torture, cannibalism, dismembering, and endless torments. Where do such terrible thoughts come from? And why do people still believe in heaven and hell, given all the evidence to the contrary?

The alarm vibrated in my jeans pocket. I dug out the phone and swiped it off. It was finally time for the tour to start. What a relief!

I left the baptistery and found my special tour group, joining them just as they entered the cathedral. The tour guide scanned the ticket on my iPhone: thirty Euros for a glimpse of Florence without the long lines.

Stepping into the cathedral I felt like I was standing on the surface of the ocean. High above me, the ceiling appeared as rows of racing sails, like parachutes. It reminded me of my attempt to kite surf in Maui. A wind-filled ceiling. Uplifting. Yet the cathedral itself was mostly bare, empty. I felt like I was standing on a surfboard in the middle of the ocean.

Behind me, I noticed a huge twenty-four hour clock at one end of the cathedral: the hours ran counterclockwise from I to XXIIII. Beside me, a painting on the wall—a life-size horse, slightly stiff, both right legs in the air, an unbalanced pose for such a large animal. I felt that the horse and rider might topple out of the painting and onto me at any moment. This is not the way horses move their legs.

I walked across floor decorations made from colored marble until I stood in front of a circular stained glass window high above the altar. The information plate stated it was created by Donatello between 1434 and 1437. It depicted the Coronation of the Virgin, Mary's elevation to glory after her death.

"Aletheia, why is mankind enamored with virgin births?"

Aletheia said that even the ancient Greeks and Romans believed in virgin births. To keep her pure, the virgin Danae's father locked her in a tower, but Zeus transformed himself into a shower of gold and entered through the roof of the tower. He got her pregnant and she gave birth to Perseus. And Mars miraculously visited the virgin Rhea Silvia and fathered Romulus and Remus. Yes, like the Christians, the ancient Greeks and Romans also believed in divine fathers, divine insemination, and miraculous births.

The tour guide led us through an interior door to a stairway, and we climbed and climbed, and then exited onto an exterior terrace. We walked a short distance with the cathedral's red roof, large red terracotta pots and a metal railing on our left, a concrete balustrade separating us from a precipitous drop on our right, and then we turned around. Directly in front of us loomed the huge, hexagonal dome of the cathedral, covered with faded red tiles. The walls of the cathedral, the supporting structures, and the myriad architectural elements were all decorated with black and white marble: black rectangles like picture frames, black striping, and black accents.

Peering over the concrete railing, I could see the baptistery roof below. Nothing impressive, except I could now discern the eight sides of the building. Undoubtedly it was the inspiration for Brunelleschi's octagonal dome. I gazed down at the tourists gathered around the baptistery, colorful umbrellas floating like flowers in a sea of black asphalt. It had drizzled while we were inside.

The countryside on this side of the cathedral appeared hilly, draped in gray clouds. Rain in the distance washed out part of our view. The horizon appeared as a thick green brush stroke, a horizontal strip of greenery, suggesting farms or vineyards or possibly orchards, and the red-tiled roofs of the city extended almost as far as the eye could see. Orderly, everything orderly, yet also old – Medieval? Renaissance?

A sudden downpour cut short my reverie: we turned and rushed back along the terrace path and into the cathedral.

Once inside, we followed our tour guide to a circular,

interior walkway, just below the great dome. Close up, we could see the vivid frescoes on the underside of the dome. I stood face-to-face with Jesus and Satan: a witness to the last judgment. Satan had two kudu-like horns and hell was pinkish-red. Demons had pointed wings and small whippet-like tails. Several carried heavy rods that were lit like torches. One demon forced a flaming rod into the anus of a man. Another set the genitals of a man on fire, or was it a woman? The devil was chewing on a half-devoured human.

Leaving the interior walkway, we entered a narrow staircase inside the dome – a dome within a dome. Narrow, no room to pass. Not a good place to be caught by zombies wearing business suits! It was a workspace left by the builders of the dome, not a space designed for tourists.

The tour group began our very slow ascent. We did not have enough room to pass or fall behind; we barely had enough room to breathe. The air was stale and warm. We all began to sweat as we climbed and our body odor hung in the air.

We reached a small ladder that led up to an opening in the floor of the stone lantern. I grabbed a water-pipe-like railing and pulled myself through the trap door. I stood upright and breathed in a lungful of fresh air, still humid from the recent rain shower.

A 360-degree view of gray sky greeted us. We were standing on top of the enormous dome! All of Florence lay before us. I studied the river Arno, the streets, the buildings, the movement of traffic and people. The buildings were no more than four or five stories. Strategically, climbing the dome had been a great idea.

And then I felt a tremor. My first thought was 'there's heavy construction nearby' and then I imagined that a large truck just passed. But there was no construction and no traffic.

"Was that an earthquake?" someone asked.

"Just a tremor," our tour guide replied. His voice was calm, indifferent to our concern. "There are minor tremors all the time."

I stepped aside from the group so I could ask, "Aletheia, does Florence, Italy have earthquakes?"

"Cogitating. OK, I found this on the web for 'does Florence Italy have earthquakes': 'Michelangelo's David to get earthquake-proof pedestal,' by Josephine McKenna, Rome, in *The Telegraph*."

I read the first paragraph of the article on my phone: "The Italian government is to spend Euros 200,000 (Pounds 160,000) on a new plinth to support Michelangelo's statute of David after hundreds of earth tremors shook Florence and the surrounding region in recent days."

Shit! Oh, shit!

Aletheia listed two other articles that I quickly skimmed: a church in central Italy had been completely destroyed in an earthquake, and a whole Italian town had collapsed. So where were the tourist alerts? Why hadn't I known? I would never have climbed to the top of an old medieval building if I had been informed!

Would the huge brick dome collapse on itself? The heavy upper layer crushing the interior dome? What were the odds that someone would be crushed? What were the odds that it would be me?

"Aletheia, is the dome in the Florence Duomo safe from earthquakes?"

"Let me think about that."

My heart beat faster as I waited for an answer. I knew

that my fight-or-flight reflex was triggering. My adrenaline was surging. My palms felt warm. Damn it! I wiped my hands on my jeans.

I also knew it was best for me to become inactive and quiet when I had an adrenaline rush, unless there was an immediate threat. Otherwise I might hurt myself or someone else.

"Aletheia, what is your conclusion?"

"Liko, I do not predict earthquakes. I did not find the necessary information to calculate if the Cathedral of Santa Maria del Fiore and its dome in Florence, Italy are safe from earthquakes."

My impulse was to flee immediately, to descend the stairs to the floor of the cathedral and run out onto the street. However, the tour guide's phrase 'many tremors' and his calm demeanor kept me in check, at least momentarily.

I hate tight spaces. Once before, while touring a WWII-era submarine, the USS Bowfin, in Honolulu, Hawaii, I had irrational thoughts about walls closing in on me. I had imagined the skin of the submarine imploding and crushing me.

And now I had to descend a medieval stairway through a brick dome after earth tremors? Damn! Common sense told me that a dome made of bricks and mortar was not an earthquake-hardened structure. And it was too late to take precautions.

Still, I knew that it would help if I allowed the adrenaline in my body to dissipate. I needed to control my breathing, too. I needed time to control myself.

It had stopped raining, at least for the present, so I could remain outside on the roof of the dome. I inhaled the moist, after-rain air.

I saw the tour guide disappearing through the trap door. I waved him goodbye and parted with the tour group. I was now alone on the roof, except for a few tourists.

To my chagrin, the group of nuns that I had seen earlier emerged through the trapdoor and fanned out on the platform. Their religious habits fluttered in the wind. I imagined a swarm of termites emerging from the ground and about to take flight.

The nuns had caught up with me because my self-inflected paralysis had rooted me to the top of the dome. I was no longer alone. I counted six nuns in full-blown religious habits. Several wore funny hats, too. Trying to force myself to relax, I Googled "funny nun hat" and learned it was called a *coif* and the separate parts were the *bandeau*, *veil*, and *wimple*.

What would I do without Aletheia? She was a steadfast companion, even during tremors.

The nuns smiled at me and I smiled at them and we all tried to be polite. Nevertheless, I pitied them for their gullible acceptance of their religious dogma. I had no doubt that some, if not all of them, believed in the human-eating Satan that I had just seen on the underside of the dome. Undoubtedly the nuns were looking forward to the Day of Judgment, that gruesome event. It saddened me to think that they looked forward to such nightmares.

Five minutes later I caught myself pacing back and forth, my stomach fluttering with butterflies. My breathing exercises were not working. Hyperventilation was only a breath away. I needed a paper sack to breathe into, to vomit into, to reassure me. I stopped and pushed my body weight against a buttress, as if I were Hercules bracing the dome against collapse. I closed my eyes. My fists pushed against mortar.

And then I felt a hand on my fist. I had a memory flash of Uncle Keahi touching my hand just as we began our descent into the belly of the USS Bowfin submarine exhibit. On that occasion my hands had been clammy. I now realized how compassionate his touch had been.

I opened my eyes, turned, and found myself face-to-face with a nun – a totally unexpected surprise. I looked into her old, clouded eyes. Her eyesight must have been poor because cataracts were obscuring her vision, at least partially. But her small hand was gently resting on my massive fist. Her comforting hand, her clouded eyes, and her kind smile all conveyed compassion.

The overall effect was similar to being shocked out of the hiccups. I was so surprised to find myself face-to-face with a wrinkled, elderly nun holding my hand that I completely forgot my irregular breathing. The surprise of her unexpected kindness literally took my breath away and reset my respiration.

"Thank you."

She smiled, nodded her head. I waited but she didn't say anything. Perhaps she didn't speak English.

In gratitude, I returned her smile. I opened my fist, took her small hand in mine, and patted the top of her weathered hand. Again, thanking her.

The other nuns took in the view of Florence, and then they gathered around their elderly sister. I found myself surrounded by nuns. I noted that my breathing was normal again and my pounding heart was quiet.

When it became clear they were going to descend, I decided it was time for me to do the same. So we descended together, passing through the trap door together. Nuns were in front of me, beside me, behind me, encouraging me with their presence every step of the way.

Me, a big six-foot-plus guy, and the nuns all shapes and sizes, but considerably smaller.

During the first part of the descent, I paused at a small exterior window long enough to gulp down air like a gold-fish confined in a narrow-necked bowl. To my surprise, a nun paused with me. I felt her genuine unspoken concern for me.

When the stairs zigzagged one time too many, when I was dizzy and short of breath again—and not because of physical exertion but because of a mounting wave of nau-sea—a heavy-set nun put her hand on my shoulder. Was her unexpected gesture to steady herself or to steady me? We both knew the answer, but neither of us said a word. My smile to her was my thank you. And then we contin-ued the descent.

When the stairs grew tighter and tighter and I could no longer turn around easily, and when I thought of the trapped sailors in the USS Arizona, and when my hands began to tremble, and my fingers tingled, the kind, elderly nun appeared again. She smiled, took my hand between her two weathered, dry hands and helped me continue my descent.

It was a surreal experience. I felt no embarrassment holding her hand part of the way down. I was as unabashed as a child holding his mother's hand. In fact, I was grateful. Hercules be damned!

We stopped one last time on the way down. She pro-duced a water bottle from some hidden pocket in her habit. My mouth was dry; I had lost my spit early on. I took a sip and then guzzled several mouthfuls of water.

"Thank you. You are very very kind."

She capped and returned the bottle to her costume. She

never said a word. I don't recall that any of the nuns said anything to me.

And then we arrived at the cathedral floor. The nuns regrouped. I thanked them with a smile and a slight bow of my head. As they departed the cathedral, the elderly nun and I waved farewell.

I was no longer nervous about the cathedral collapsing. I sat down at one of the pews available for the tourists and took out my iPhone.

"Aletheia, please send an email to Mrs. Eyles."

"Yes, Liko."

"Dear Mrs. Eyles, Today a group of nuns taught me an important lesson. The lesson was about compassion. What the world needs is compassionate common sense. Not just truth. Not just compassion. Truth and compassion should stand together, hand in hand. The world would be a much better place if they did. Your student, Liko."

And there was another lesson learned, too, a lesson about claustrophobia. I knew for a fact, now, that tight spaces, dark narrow spaces, make me claustrophobic. That was also a very good thing to know.

The origin of my claustrophobia was undoubtedly the disastrous quarry dive that had occurred two and a half years earlier in Nevada. A young girl had drowned and I held myself responsible because I failed to alert her to the hazardous conditions in the water. My claustrophobia grew out of the nightmares that followed her drowning: dreams of cold, dark, deep water—and zero visibility.

My ticket included a special visit to the crypt. Before descending, I wondered whose bones I would see. Aletheia provided me a biblical reference about bones in the Old Testament, from 2 Kings: "So Elisha died, and they buried him. Now bands of Moabites used to invade the land in the spring of the year. And as a man was being buried, lo, a marauding band was seen and the man was cast into the grave of Elisha: and as soon as the man touched the bones of Elisha, he revived, and stood to his feet."

Now that was an unabashed miracle performed by God. The Bible's message? All you need is contact with the relics of a saint. Today, the Catholic pantheon of saints includes St. George in England, St. Andrew in Scotland, St. Martin in France, St. Bridget in Ireland, St. Catherine in Italy, and St. Mark in Venice. A pagan smorgasbord.

Fortunately, there were no narrow dark stairs so I quickly walked down the open staircase into a museum-like area. Elisha was not in the crypt, but I was not disappointed. The relics were awesome! All kinds of body parts: fingers, legs, kneecaps, everything imaginable. They say St. Catherine's head is a relic somewhere in Sienna, too.

Once I exited the crypt and was outside the cathedral, I sat down with Aletheia and we perused the Bible looking for verses about the power of relics. She shared Matthew 9:20-22, Acts 5:14-16, and Acts 19:11-12: A woman touched the hem of Christ's cloak and was healed of a hemorrhage, Peter's shadow passed over the sick and they were healed, and Paul's handkerchiefs and clothing healed the sick and exorcised evil spirits.

I believe death is final. This life is all there is. There is no immortality. I am a conscious being, and there is no consciousness after death. I accept that. Fortunately an earthquake had not taken me this afternoon.

My Canali suit fitted me perfectly. I stared in the mirror

at my flat-front pants and double vented jacket. It was just what I wanted. And I liked the real horn buttons, too. Even the shoes were comfortable. The gray-haired gentleman in the shoe department did have to stretch the leather for my oversized left foot, though. My left foot was a half-inch longer than my right, making it impossible to find a pair of shoes that perfectly fit both feet. But I was happy with the shiny black shoes and their narrow tied laces.

I looked at my physical build. Today I was proud of my genes. I looked healthy and strong, and the suit was a perfect fit.

"A personal tip, sir." The gray-haired salesman reached around me from behind and unbuttoned the bottom button of the jacket. "Only button the top, never the bottom."

"Thank you." I turned sideways and surveyed myself in the suit. I was wearing the gray suit with white shirt and tie. "Very nice."

I noted the beautiful symmetry. I thought the suit looked great, and that made me happy. "Exquisite craftsmanship," I said.

"Thank you, sir."

It was seldom that I felt such pride, self-respect, and strength.

And then I thought of the kind, elderly nun, and the costume that she had been wearing. I thought of my weakness and her kindness. I gently slapped my right hand into the palm of my left and squeezed my hands together, remembering how she had helped me. Did anything like that happen to Hercules, or Perseus, or . . . probably not.

It was time to return to my hotel and prepare for the gala dinner. I hoped finally to meet the mystery woman. But what if the men who assaulted her showed up?

Back in my hotel, nervous, I spent time with Aletheia, learning about CRISPR. I thought it might be useful if cornered and forced to make small talk, cocktail conversation. What I discovered about CRISPR-Cas9 was that I should take a class in genetics when I get to university.

The acronym CRISPR made no more sense than its individual words: clustered regularly interspaced short palindromic repeats. Really? I had no idea, even after looking it up, what "palindromic repeats" were. I discovered that Cas9 was a protein that researchers used to cut DNA as if they wielded a scalpel. Cas9 was essentially a precise gene-snipping tool, so scientists use CRISPR Cas9 to remove and replace genes. Researchers could use CRISPR on any creature, even humans. It allowed the mixing and matching of pieces of DNA within an individual, between two people, for an entire species, or between one or more species. Some had likened it to Microsoft Word software commands that enable users to cut, copy, and replace words, phrases, and even paragraphs. I imagined it more like evolutionary Lego pieces for researchers, age 13 and above.

I was nervous because I knew that I was out of my league here. I might as well crash an awards dinner for brain surgeons. And I was too young to pass for anything more than a graduate student, so that was my ploy. Tonight I would be an excited research student seeking an internship. Would that work? I wondered.

I had studied in my boxer shorts, but I had kept my dress shirt and tie on because I wasn't sure that I could re-tie the tie. I had never worn one before. There was no need for a tie in Hawaii, and my mother and I never went to church or any dress-up events in Las Vegas. So I pulled on my dress pants, used the shoehorn to slip into my black dress shoes, and tied the black laces. I then donned the jacket.

I paused and looked at myself in the mirror. I adjusted the tie. I didn't look as great as Schwarzenegger in *True Lies*, but the Canali suit was impressive. It would still be a miracle, though, if I pulled this off tonight.

After breakfast this morning, I had snooped around the conference message board, hoping to learn the name of the mystery woman. I had not been that fortunate. Nevertheless, I had learned something else of value. One of the speakers was sick and his afternoon session had been cancelled. I hoped that he would be too ill to attend the dinner tonight, too, especially since I intended to use his name to gain entry. The staff would either have a list of guests or they would be handing out nametags. Either way, I was now prepared. Tonight I was Dr. E. O. Harrison. There was one catch: I didn't know if the E stood for Everett or Ellen. I smiled, thinking about that.

Was the mystery woman here? Had she arrived on the coach transfer from the St. Regis Hotel to the Palazzo Capponi All'Annunziata? Was she coming for the cocktail reception, or just the dinner? How would she react when she saw me?

Those were the questions churning in my mind as I approached the main entrance of the Baroque palace. The long, horizontal façade of the three-story palace projected power, victory and control. The main entrance opened into an enormous reception area and a dramatic muscular staircase. My eyes surveyed the Baroque paintings that lined the walls and the frescoes that covered the ceiling.

The artwork exploded in intense color, emotion, and tension. What I could see, I liked a lot.

I stopped at the reception table. I scanned the nametags spread out alphabetically on the table and I pointed to the nametag for Dr. E. O. Harrison. The woman behind the table picked it up and handed it to me. Hopefully Dr. Harrison was still sick and would not show up later.

"Is the dinner assigned seating?"

"No, Dr. Harrison. You are free to sit where you like."

"Thank you."

I turned and stepped towards the grand stairway. I then paused for a moment and feigned pinning Dr. Harrison's nametag to my coat. Instead I slipped it into my inner coat pocket and I smiled. I now had free access to the palace and dinner and, most especially, the mystery woman. But where was she?

As I ascended the grand Baroque staircase, hoping to gain a higher vantage point to survey the crowd of guests and to look for any suspicious men in suits, the spectacular ceiling fresco stunned me. I was witness to Olympus and the Labors of Hercules. I found it refreshing after all the Christian religious art.

I like Hercules. He reminds me of my Uncle Keahi and his great physical strength. My uncle is a weight lifter in Waikiki. He is taller and stronger than me. I admire him. He saved my life twice: once when we were snorkeling and the second time during a night dive.

I identify with Hercules. I read all the stories and myths about him. He was incredibly strong, but he was also extremely proud and easily offended, like me. He was very emotional too, also like me. He behaved foolishly and then had to perform great deeds to redeem himself. I feel like

I'm on that same path. Like Hercules, I create my own problems.

I stopped halfway up the grand staircase. Below me was a fountain with statues of Mercury, Venus, and Apollo. Great characters, great Roman myths. Nobody believes in them today. I suspect that will happen to the Abrahamic religions, too. One day the Jewish, Christian, and Islamic religions will be as dead as these Greek and Roman gods. The mighty religions of today will be recognized for what they are: myths and mythology. And then everyone will be able to enjoy the cathedrals and religious art for what they are, just as I do. But the repetition does get boring.

I entered the gallery of the Palazzo Capponi. Again, I had done my homework before arriving, with Aletheia's assistance. The palace was the former home of Senator Capponi, who died in 1760, just before the American Revolution. At the time the palace was built, Captain Kidd was hung in London and Benjamin Franklin was born in Boston. During its construction, Spain lost control of Italy and Austria was becoming a major player. A hundred years later, Napoleon would crown himself Emperor of Italy. Napoleon was entertained and dined here, and now, two hundred years later, it was my turn.

A woman walked by and smiled at me. I noticed her back was slightly arched, as I had seen a woman arch her back not long ago. Nice breasts! I watched her hips sway gently as she walked away. Wow! I wondered—is it my new Canali suit?

When I entered the main hall, I saw a coat of arms. Was it the coat of arms of the Capponi family? And portraits, probably of the Capponi family. I read the information plate for a large painting: Pier Capponi, received by Charles VIII.

I think religious politicians are strongly nationalistic and like attacking other countries. That's something that both President Bush and the Ayatollah Khomeini had in common. I'd try to remember to ask Aletheia about it later.

I watched two men in business suits embrace and pat each other on the back. They greeted two women, kissed them high on their cheeks, first right, then left, a cultural ritual I had been introduced to when I met my great-aunt in Hawaii several years ago. I wondered if she learned it here in Italy?

Where was the mystery woman?

I strolled around and mingled, but I did not see her. Time passed and it was soon 8pm. The cocktail reception was ending and I felt deeply disappointed, so I wandered into the dining room.

I saw a woman flirting with a man. She gave him a coy look, cocked her head and then looked up shyly at him. She arched her back, breasts forward, and tossed her hair. I watched another couple stare intently at each other for several seconds. Were they aware that they were staring at each other? They dropped their stare, and then the woman smiled and looked directly at him. He smiled, too. Open, happy smiles, both flashing white teeth.

It seemed that everywhere I went, men and women were meeting, sizing each other up, pairing off. So far I had met no one. So far I had no friend, no fellow adventurer, no lover. Aletheia was a tool, not a companion. Only zombies in business suits pursued me.

And then there she was! The mystery woman! She was seated at a table with the men who had doted on her during breakfast.

Why was my heart racing? I rubbed my hands together. My palms were damp so I dried them on my dress pants, stroking my thighs up and down until I become conscious of my bad manners.

I now noticed the band, either because the stocky bass player lost the tempo, or the kick drum and snare wandered off pace. My heart skipped a beat, too. Time was no longer solid. I was nervous.

Without thinking, I walked across the room towards her table. Halfway across, I realized that I was going to join her. I took a deep breath. I had decided to sit at her table.

As I approached, I was conscious that I was playing with the shirt cuff on my right arm. I turned back the cuff to reveal a gold bracelet, the only piece of jewelry I owned. I had bought it for myself as a reward for joining the swim team and learning how to swim during my senior high school year, and for following through on my resolution to lift weights and lose weight. I had spent my earnings from working after school at the Steak House on this bracelet. I was fortunate to be able to afford it, largely thanks to my great-aunt, because she agreed to cover all my travel and other post-graduation expenses. I was aware that I was preening as I approached the woman. I asked myself why I was doing this?

I stood, uninvited, across the table from her, my hands on the back of a chair. I could see recognition in her eyes. An astonished hazel gaze.

I felt myself stand tall, shift from foot to foot. I sensed that she was waiting for me to move, to say something, to make time physical.

The man on my right extended his hand, "I'm Dr. Keyes."

"I'm Liko Koholua. May I join you?" I couldn't believe

that I had just used my real first name. But then, telling the truth comes natural to me. I did use my mother's maiden name, though.

I shook Dr. Keyes' hand. He barely gripped mine. A limp handshake.

My first impression of Dr. Keyes was that he was a she. His eyes were piercing blue, his lips pouty, his blond hair shoulder-length. He was so feminine that I must have gawked with surprise. That embarrassed me. I thought he caught my embarrassment and liked it.

The other two men at the table extended their hands and told me their names, but I didn't hear any of it, because I was not listening. I was waiting for the woman to talk, to do something.

As I took her hand in mine, she said, "My name is Istina."

"The Queen of Genetics," Mr. Keyes quipped, smiling.

"Istina?" I gave her a slight nod and released her hand. I then sat myself next to Dr. Keyes, the only vacant seat at the table. In the next minute I almost knocked over a glass of red wine, then my glass of water. I drew my arms and then my hands back into my body. I made smaller gestures. I tried to relax. What did I have to prove here? I just wanted information. An understanding.

It was too noisy to hear anyone except my immediate neighbors: Dr. Keyes on my right, and a man in an Armani suit on my left. I could see Istina's ruby lips move but I couldn't hear the words. It was just too damn noisy! The small band was playing, and everyone at every table was buzzing with chatter and small talk. I disliked it, immensely. Had I made a mistake?

I leaned towards Dr. Keyes and started a conversation, first about the weather and then about the Vasari Corridor. I mentioned the 1993 bombing. He wasn't interested. Instead he talked about the self-portraits collection in the corridor: donations to the Medici family and the Uffizi gallery by the painters themselves—between 1,000 and 1,500 paintings, he said. He knew a lot about art. I knew nothing. I'd heard of Rembrandt, but I'd never seen one. He talked about Velaquez and Delacroix and Ensor, but I had no idea who they were.

I guessed that Dr. Keyes was in his late 40s. He struck me as an androgynous model, not a researcher. He was medium height, skinny, and pretty-faced. I imagined him modeling for an artist or appearing on the cover of a men's fashion magazine. I couldn't imagine him in a laboratory.

I sipped the red wine and sat back and looked closer at Dr. Keyes. His blue suit fit him well—impeccable tailoring. And he wore a navy blue neck scarf instead of a tie. The blue accentuated the blue in his eyes. I thought that he had an unflattering awareness of his beauty.

Dr. Keyes said, "The most interesting panel today was on the possibilities of resurrecting extinct species, including the woolly mammoths."

"And Neanderthal people," the man on my left, wearing the Armani suit, added.

The two men talked across me and I listened. They discussed the creation of extinct species banks, whatever that was. I worried that their spittle was falling on my dinnerware.

The Armani suit stated: "I liked the panel on the creation of man and animal and plant hybrids."

"Chimeras?" Dr. Keyes imitated a Peter Lorre voice as he said: "Creatures made from human body parts AND animals AND plants. Now that's spooky."

"What did you think about Professor Kroll's presentation?" the suit asked.

"Using the pig appendix as an organ to grow human tissues?"

"Yes, he's still looking for investors."

"Then he's still an idiot," Dr. Keyes stated, matter-of-factly.

I wondered: why was he an idiot? So, curious, I just had to ask, "Why not use pig appendixes?"

Dr. Keyes stared at me, a long stare as if he was taking the measure of me: who I was, what planet I was from, and why I was sitting next to him. The first thing I said at the table and it was a major faux pas. I felt like a game show contestant who had just lost all his points.

It was the Armani suit who answered my question, though, slowly and curtly. "Unlike humans, pigs do not have appendixes."

"However," Dr. Keyes interjected, "Professor Kroll believes that pigs still have the genes to produce an appendix; the genes are just latent, unexpressed."

"Yes," the suit agreed, nodding his head. "He believes that pigs have unexpressed vestigial genes for a non-existent vestigial appendix."

"Nicely said," Dr. Keyes smiled with a slight nod of his head.

The suit smiled, too, accepting the compliment and pleased with his wordplay. He then continued: "Second, Professor Kroll needs Istina's toolkit so he can activate, regulate and express those latent genes and regenerate a pig appendix."

Dr. Keyes added: "Istina may or may not be agreeable to that."

The suit: "Third, Professor Kroll wants to insert human

genes into the pig genome. Later the human genes would express themselves in the pig appendix."

Dr. Keyes: "His goal is to create hybrid human-pig tissue and human-pig organs."

The suit: "For tissue and organ transplants."

I asked: "You said that Professor Kroll needs Istina's toolkit?"

The Armani suit: "Yes, he needs Istina's toolkit in order to work the magic."

I looked at Istina. She was talking to the third man at the table, the man sitting directly across from me and on her right, but she was speaking in a low voice and the third man was mumbling. I wished that I could hear what they were saying.

There was nothing remarkable about the third man, except he was wearing sunglasses that made him look pretentious. They were a John Lennon style, round, gray lenses in a gunmetal black frame. Why wear sunglasses indoors at dinner? Were his eyes sensitive to light? Or was he infamous and in hiding? Whatever the reason, it was annoying.

I asked Dr. Keyes, "So, why not?"

"Why not what?" he retorted.

"Why doesn't Istina let him use her toolkit?"

Dr. Keyes stared at me, taken aback by my question. "She has ethical concerns with Professor Kroll's research. And Istina controls the toolkit. She owns the patent on regeneration."

"The patent on Cas9?" I asked. As soon as I asked the question, I sensed that her research must be so novel and exceptional that everyone at the conference, and definitely everyone here at the table, was familiar with it. I sensed that I had just made another major faux pas, but I was here tonight to get answers.

"Others own the patent on Cas9. Istina's patent is different. It's a novel regeneration tool, although it was developed using Cas9."

I thought to myself: you guys have had way too much wine. You've seen one science fiction movie too many. Besides, it doesn't sound safe to me. Was this why Istina and the man were almost kidnapped? Or murdered?

Dinner was then served. The individual menu that accompanied my place setting guided me through the courses: eggplant and mozzarella cheese millefeuilles, parmigiano and pureed sweet potatoes, beef fillet with Mediterranean aromas, crunchy potatoes and sage, and baby spinach with raisin and pine nuts. And from the wine cellar: Vermentino IGT Poggio Angelica Jacopo Banti, Chianti Classico D.O.C.G. Borgo Salcetino, and Water San Felice Acqua di Toscana.

I made a mental note to slow down on the wine. I determined to stay sober, self-assured, poised. I deftly folded and then placed the small menu into my inside coat pocket. I strained, determined to listen to the conversation across the table.

And then the band took a break and we could finally hear each another.

Istina said in a loud voice: "Liko, didn't we meet in Rome?"

Stunned, all I could do was slowly nod my head up and down in disbelief at her question.

"I don't recall why you were visiting Rome. Was it your family?"

"No. I was visiting the Ludus Magnus, a gladiator training center near the Colosseum."

"Oh yes, that is where we met, at the Colosseum/Roman Forum metro station, correct?"

"Yes," I replied. Of course I knew that we had met at a quieter metro station, not the Colosseum/Roman Forum.

"They still train gladiators?" Dr. Keyes asked.

I smiled while focusing on Istina's hazel eyes. "No. Gladiator combat was outlawed in the fifth century. The Ludus Magnus is the ruins of one of the greatest training centers."

"What is there to see?" Dr. Keyes pursued.

"Barracks, tiny sleeping cells, a tunnel connecting the Colosseum to the school. Fountains. A wooden post where they practiced combat."

"Rather boring?" Dr. Keyes stated, matter-of-factly.

"Not the movie," Istina interjected. "The movie *Gladiator* was exciting!"

"I'm sure," Dr. Keyes said, his voice condescending.

"It won Academy Awards," I said. I wanted to ask Aletheia for details, but I didn't think it appropriate, here at the dinner table. "I think Best Picture. Russell Crowe got Best Actor for playing Maximus Decimus Meridius."

Istina didn't say anything, so I added: "Maximus was fictitious." Everyone at the table was listening to me now. Embarrassed, I forged ahead. "But Commodus was real. And his father, Marcus Aurelius, too."

Still, silence from the table. "They were real, but Ridley Scott fictionalized them."

"How so?" Istina asked.

"In the movie, Commodus murders his father, smothers him. But in real life his father died of smallpox." I smiled, hopeful that my monologue would end well. "And Commodus didn't die in the arena, killed by Russell Crowe.

In real life, he was strangled taking a bath by a wrestler named Narcissus, who was his personal trainer."

Istina grimaced. "People prefer embellishments, exaggerations. Drama."

I could feel my breath catch between my throat and lungs as I gazed at her. Her hazel eyes were beautiful. Who the hell was she? She was a researcher. She held a cutting-edge patent that was used to regenerate tissues and organs. She was opposed to mixing human and animal genes. Why did someone attack her?

I replied. "Yes. And lately I have spent a lot of time separating fact from fiction here in Florence, too. In the churches. A lot of Catholic drama here. A lot of myth."

Dr. Keyes asked, "Liko. That's your name, right? Liko?"

"Yes." I noted that I was the only person at the table who was not wearing a name badge. And ironically, they all knew each other. I considered taking Dr. E. O. Harrison's name badge out of my pocket and pinning it to my coat pocket, declaring myself a doctor. But now, seated with real researchers, scientists with real PhDs, I realized that hadn't been the brightest idea. Besides, someone here at the table undoubtedly knew him. And I had already introduced myself using my real name.

"Where did you do your studies, and what is your research?"

My heart jumped a beat.

I glanced at Istina and the man seated next to her. Istina appeared suddenly nervous. The man next to her in the round sunglasses was unreadable, a mystery. I guessed that was one advantage of wearing sunglasses. His appearance annoyed me, though. Men with round faces should wear square glasses. His face was round.

The man in the Armani suit looked at me questioningly.

With that simple question, 'What is your research?' Dr. Keyes had outed me.

But then Dr. Keyes placed his hand under the table and on my leg. He patted my thigh. He then placed both of his hands on the table in front of him. He had outed me, yet this unexpected gesture was his way of telling me that it was okay. The pat on the thigh and his smile said: "*Yes, I am outing you, you do not belong here, but I will not draw blood.*"

So I confessed, "Well, I just graduated high school. I haven't started my studies yet."

"So why are you here? Are you a protester?"

"No."

"A reporter?"

"No."

"So…?"

"To learn." I decided to be honest, as honest as I could be under the circumstances. "I'm curious."

"Really?"

"Your passion is genetics? Mine is the ocean. I love biology. Someday I will attend university and study marine biology. It won't hurt to know something about genetics."

Dr. Keyes looked at me closely; his blue eyes drilled into mine. "So why are you here?"

"I stumbled upon the conference. This new tool, CRISPR, it caught my attention."

I glanced at Istina. She looked like she was just short of having a full-blown nervous attack. I guess my presence at her table, and how poorly I had managed the meeting with her, and her coworkers, was upsetting.

And then the man in the sunglasses announced to the table: "Tomorrow is the last day of our conference. We leave the day after tomorrow."

I thought to myself, *That leaves me very little time.*

I looked across the table at Istina. I lifted my glass of red wine to my lips and took a sip. I caught my breath again when she smoothed her hair.

Her hair again reminded me of strands of pulled licorice taffy. I love licorice. As a kid, my mom made taffy candy from scratch. She stirred licorice extract into a sugar syrup, and then boiled it into a hard ball. Mom and I rubbed oil on our hands so the sugar would not stick and burn. We worked the hard ball of taffy until it was pliable, pulling it, folding it, twisting it into black strands. I wondered: Does Istina's hair smell of sea salt and ocean and sugar?

"What do you want with her?" Dr. Keyes asked me, in a low voice. He had caught me staring at Istina. I was thankful, though, that he had finally lowered his voice.

But I didn't answer. How could I say, "I want to know why I killed a man in Rome?"

Dr. Keyes smiled. He nodded his head towards Istina and then looked at me. "She is pretty, isn't she?"

I thought I was blushing. I looked at him and furrowed my eyebrows. I nodded yes.

I looked back across the table at Istina. She rolled her eyes. She had heard Dr. Keyes' question. Perhaps she had been listening to our conversation all along. She and Dr. Keyes looked at each other and she shook her head side to side, her way of telling him 'enough.' He pursed his pouty lips and nodded, okay.

Just as suddenly as I had been outed, now no one was interested in me. They began to talk among themselves and ignored me. I had lost all credibility, anyway. I was the uninvited guest who had crashed a dinner party and had been discovered. The Armani suit and the man in the sunglasses now gave me the cold shoulder. Everyone did.

The conversation shifted; it seemed no one at the table had attended the plenary session on transhumanism and religion. Everyone was more interested in new innovations in genetic tools and methods. For myself, I did not know enough about the CRISPR technology to have a reasoned opinion about it. I hoped that CRISPR would make our species stronger, smarter, and healthier, but I needed more information.

The band returned from their recess and began to play again. People finished their main courses and waited for dessert. Conversations were renewed and the room gradually grew noisy again.

Istina excused herself from the table and went to the bathroom. It was the opportunity I had been waiting for. After a minute I excused myself, too. I ambushed her when she stepped out of the women's room.

"What happened in Rome?"

She started to walk past me but I stepped in front of her. "There is a private garden. We can talk there."

"No," she said. "It is better, safer, if I stay with the group."

"What happened—"

"They were after my brother."

"They weren't after you?"

"No. It is my brother that they really want."

"Why?"

She exhaled deeply and shook her head. She countered my question. "Why are you here?" Her adult eyes measured me, gauged my age, my youth. She added, "No one knows who you are." She looked around. I did too. No one else was in the hallway with us. "No one knows that you killed the man. Or did you talk to the police?"

"No, I didn't talk to the police."

"Then don't." She glanced over my shoulder and suddenly raised her voice and changed the subject: "Yes, our table is too close to the band. It's much too noisy."

I glanced over my shoulder, too. The man with the sunglasses had just walked up behind me.

"Let's talk later," I suggested.

She frowned and shook her head.

I didn't know how to interpret the shake of her head. Was she refusing to see me again or was she admonishing me for being foolish? For not just disappearing?

"After dinner," I suggested to her.

But she shook her head, no.

I walked down the hall to the men's room. The third man followed me.

He and I stood beside each other at the urinals, but neither of us said a word. We kept our eyes straight ahead on the marble walls. I let him finish and wash his hands first, and when he left the restroom I stared at myself in the mirror for a moment, collecting my thoughts. It wasn't going as I had hoped. In fact, it wasn't going well at all—but at least no one had thrown me out. The bottom line, I guessed, was that they thought that I was just a young kid who crashed their dinner. At best I was entertainment, and at worst I was disrupting serious conversation about research. But they knew each other well, so I was a momentary distraction, maybe entertainment. I was handsome, polite, curious, and honest, so why would they report me? My meal wasn't costing them anything. Maybe they could identify with a young kid on an adventure?

When I returned to the table, the rest of the dinner

passed slowly, boringly. I remained quiet and asked no more questions. I just listened to them talk and talk and talk about their craft.

Istina was obviously passionate about genes and genetic engineering: the mysteries of the micro-world, the laboratory. I thought it would be boring to be confined to a laboratory for so many hours, night and day. Tedious!

My passion was the ocean: the mysteries of the macro-world, animals, and their environment. Istina and I saw the world from two different viewpoints. She preferred the laboratory, while I preferred ecosystems. How compatible was that? Besides, she was considerably older, already middle-aged.

Dessert was served—a small black cake with chocolate foam and fresh raspberries, parfait, and cubes of apricot with pistachio from Bronte. Istina had a small samovar of coffee, and then dinner was over.

Everyone was polite but somewhat aloof now. I had been embarrassed so many times in my life that tonight was just par for the course. I guess crashing the dinner had been a dumb idea. Something that Hercules would have done. I smiled.

My Canali suit no longer felt comfortable. It now felt fake. I sighed and loosened the pink tie. I unbuttoned the top shirt button. The dress shoes now pinched my feet. I couldn't wait to change my clothes and put my jeans and T-shirt and sandals back on.

When Istina pushed her chair away from the table and stood up, her colleagues were immediately around her. The secret service could not have provided a better buffer between her and the world, including me. Her colleagues were like drones protecting a queen bee. I hadn't noticed this before. Perhaps they weren't even aware of it, either.

They moved as a group through the dining hall, pausing to acknowledge a colleague, to shake hands with a fellow researcher, to comment favorably about the dinner and palace. I walked with them to the main entrance. Dr. Keyes helped Istina into her magenta coat and they stepped out into the formal courtyard.

I said goodbye to Istina as she and her coworkers met the coach to return to the St. Regis Hotel. I stepped forward, past Dr. Keyes, and boldly kissed her on the cheek. I whispered, "I'll see you at breakfast tomorrow."

"No," she said. To my surprise it was an emphatic 'no.' And it was loud enough for everyone nearby to hear, including Dr. Keyes and the man in the Armani suit. The third man just stared at me through those sunglasses.

After the last person stepped aboard the coach, the man wearing the sunglasses said something to the driver. I watched as he got off the bus and walked over to me.

He stepped up to me and stopped in my personal space, his body less than a foot in front of me. I smelled his body: he was wearing musk. He tilted his head back and his round sunglasses looked up at me, black with a gray gradient. The sunglasses were Prada. He leaned in. I smelled his breath: red wine.

"If I see you again I will call the polizia." A short pause. "Understood?"

I bit my tongue. What I wanted to do was punch him in the face.

He walked back to the coach. I guessed he was five feet eleven inches tall and 180 pounds. He was not a serious physical threat, but he had just threatened me. He quickly re-boarded the coach and the group drove away.

I wished I had broken his nose! Right then and there I decided that the next time I saw him I'd take his sunglasses. I recalled how some asshole like him had stolen my sunglasses during my first week in Waikiki, right off my towel on the beach. He was that kind of an asshole. Yep, it was time I got my sunglasses back. I knew that didn't quite make sense, yet it did.

As I walked back to my hotel I replayed everything said, every gesture, every detail I could remember. Slowly I overcame the embarrassment of being outed. I was pissed at my lack of planning, though. I had only myself to blame for not getting answers from the mystery woman.

But I was stubborn. Tomorrow morning I was going to see Istina again. I was going to see her alone. I was going to get some answers.

5

As I approached Istina's hotel I saw a blue police van and three policemen wearing blue football-like helmets. I also spotted several men in suits with earbuds plugged in.

In the center of the piazza I could see American protesters. They were easy to identify: baseball hats, clean New Balance shoes, proud stomachs hanging over narrow belts. They were pasty-skinned and sun-deprived. I saw an occasional black-bound Bible, so they were probably evangelical Christians, too. Their signs were the final giveaway: "DON'T PLAY GOD."

The white American evangelical protesters had formed their own small group, separate from the Italian protesters who were here yesterday, maybe because of a language and cultural barrier. The Italian men were leaner and dressed better. Sometimes it was embarrassing to be an American. Even the eclectic group of researchers attending the conference looked healthier. Today I'll pretend to be Canadian.

I should have worn my suit. If I had worn my suit then I would look like someone who belonged inside the hotel and not someone who belonged in the protest. I would be less conspicuous in a suit. But I was too embarrassed after last night.

As I walked across the piazza, a policeman stopped me. "Can I help you?"

"No. I'm meeting someone in the Winter Garden Restaurant ... for breakfast." It was a truthful statement because my intention was to find Istina and ask her on a date, kind of. I knew that was a crazy thing to do after last night, but I had made up my mind. I wanted to know about the man that I had killed, and Istina had the answers. Today was the last day of the conference and my last chance to talk to her.

"You are American?"

I guess my accent gave me away. "Yes."

"You are with the protesters."

I almost said 'Do I look like a white evangelical protester?' but I controlled myself. "No. I'm not with them."

"Who are you meeting?"

I wanted to say 'none of your business' but then I remembered I was not in America. Maybe they did things differently in Italy. "A friend. A woman."

He called over to his companion. "I have a young American here who wants to see his girlfriend. What do you think? Should I let him through?"

His companion was a heavy-set woman dressed in a blue police uniform. "Just a moment." She walked over and joined us. "You are here to see a woman?"

"For breakfast. And then maybe the Bargello."

She looked me up and down. Was she deciding whether I was a protester or not?

"No flowers?"

I felt my face warm. I must have been blushing. And that

was my ticket in—a blush. I was lucky. I suspected that next time it wouldn't be so easy.

Alone again at my table-for-four on the balcony overlooking the Winter Garden restaurant. Why did the waiters always seat me at the same table? Or was this paranoia, too? I'd had a sleepless night. I was tired.

I ordered a second cappuccino and then decided to descend upon the buffet in the Winter Garden, below. The waitress asked if I would prefer a table downstairs and I agreed. I hoped Istina would be there.

I took a series of deep breaths, deliberately, slowly. What was happening to me?

Last night she had encouraged me to disappear. She said no one knew who I was. She was correct. She said I didn't have to get involved. Again she was correct. Common sense told me to just slip away. So why didn't I?

I followed the waiter down the stairs. I could now smell the buffet. I had made a good choice. And then I saw her. She and her companion from last night, the guy with the Prada sunglasses, were returning to their table. He was again wearing the round sunglasses. His plate was overloaded with food. Her portions were much less. Who wore sunglasses indoors during breakfast?

I stepped out from behind the waiter and walked directly to her table. She did not smile. I noticed her lips were nude and not dark berry this morning. She was wearing a gloss, or maybe just a lip balm. I caught myself and stopped just short of staring.

Dr. Keyes also arrived at the table just as I did. He was balancing a plate full of bacon and eggs benedict and a small plate of croissants and breads. He sat down and arranged his plates. How could someone so skinny eat so much? This morning he wore a light blue scarf wrapped around his neck. What a character!

His piercing blue eyes looked up at me with dismay.

The man in the sunglasses said, "Mr. Koholua, I warned you last night." His voice was deep and carried across the dining room. "If you do not leave immediately, I will call hotel security."

I stood my ground. That is something I had learned in the trailer park: never give in to a bully. It empowers them. Besides, what I was doing would only take a minute.

I reached out and snatched the sunglasses off his round face. I put them on.

Shocked, he abruptly crumbled into his seat.

I gave Dr. Keyes a half-hearted smile and then turned to Istina. "Good morning Istina. How are you this morning?"

Istina looked at me as if I was crazy. Then she glanced at the man without his sunglasses to see how he was reacting to my cheerful indifference to his warning. He was staring at me in disbelief.

Dr. Keyes sat with his back straight, smiling. I could tell he liked drama.

Istina turned back to me. "I'm very well, thank you." The tone of her voice said I was not welcome.

"I'm going to the Bargello today." I hoped I pronounced Bargello right. "Join me?"

She hesitated and averted her eyes from my gaze—a slight gesture that stopped my pulse. She had surprised me last night when she fearlessly spoke up and asked me questions about myself. But now her boldness had faded.

"Join me. Skip the conference today."

She looked up and our eyes meet.

I felt a little dizzy.

"You can't possibly miss this morning," the man without the sunglasses interjected. "We need you. We can't do the panel discussion without you."

The effect on Istina was immediate, as if he had whisked her physically away. She mentally reentered the world of academia and the conference. A place where I couldn't follow, where I couldn't compete. Did I lose her that easily?

"Besides," the man added, "it's safer inside." His tone was curt and unfriendly. "You saw the protestors." He then turned and glared at me.

Istina glanced at me, too, as if I should understand. And then she glanced at the man and nodded her head.

I formed a fist with my right hand. I was ready to step forward and break his nose. He must have known it, because he didn't move. He said to her, "If you think we should call security then I will."

"No need. I'm leaving. Istina, I'll be at the Bargello in case you change your mind." And with that I smiled the best I could, turned around, and left.

I was disappointed. Last night she seemed self-assured and brave and forceful. Had I misjudged her? Now she was timid and easily swayed. She had refused to talk with me last night and she declined to go with me now.

Walking through the restaurant wearing the Prada sunglasses gave a whole new atmosphere to everything. It imparted a false calm.

I noticed, though, that another man got up quickly from his breakfast when I passed his table. He hadn't finished his breakfast, but he tossed cash on his table and followed me through the lobby and then outdoors.

We passed the hotel porter, crossed the lobby, and exited the building. The Prada sunglasses shielded my eyes from the bright Florence sunlight. No rain today. The stranger was right on my heels.

I turned to confront him. I turned around so fast, and he was so close behind, that he bumped into me.

He said, "Are you American?"

"No. Canadian." It was a joke, but I immediately regretted it because it was also a lie. "Yes, I'm American."

The expression on his face was puzzlement, so I explained. "Those obese, obnoxious, in-your-face, white, evangelical Christians over there," I paused and gestured toward the group of protesters wearing baseball hats—one of the hats actually said 'Make America Great Again'—"they're Americans. They're an embarrassment."

"An embarrassment?"

"Yes. An embarrassment to me, to America and to the human race."

He smiled, nodding his head. "People who lock in their position annoy me, too."

Now I was puzzled. "And you are?"

"Me? A protester?"

I looked at his blue jeans, worn leather jacket, pale brown shirt, and scuffed hiking boots. "Well, you ARE dressed for a protest, not a conference."

"But I'm not with that group." He gestured at the evangelical Americans.

"Really?"

"Heaven's no! For me it's not religious. It's a matter of science. I'm a scientist."

I was now skeptical, and I almost quoted Einstein, flippantly: "Science is a wonderful thing if one does not have to earn one's living at it." But I didn't. Instead, I asked in a matter-of-fact, non-aggressive tone, "You have a science degree?"

"Oh yes. I have PhDs in biochemistry, education, and evolutionary biology from Duke and Stanford."

I pursed my lips and nodded my head. Was this guy a nut? "Wow, now that's impressive. I've never met anyone with three PhDs."

"Well, I kind of cheated on my PhD in education." He paused for a moment, for effect. "I wrote a book on evolutionary biology. Writing the book counted towards my PhD in Education. And the book summarized my evolutionary biology dissertation. So I got two PhDs for one."

His smile was so big and open that I almost laughed. Must be nice to earn a double PhD.

I extended my hand. "I am Liko."

"Jan. I'm French." We shook hands. "Nice sunglasses," he added. His smile was now a mischievous grin.

"Thanks," I replied. I thought the round Pradas looked good on my oval face.

I wondered how many languages Jan spoke. I am acutely aware that I know English and only English. I imagine this man standing in front of me knew French, English, Italian and probably other languages, too. I wondered if Aletheia could translate real time. I'd check later.

"Jan, I'm new to the topic of CRISPR."

"So, you haven't made up your mind yet about genetic engineering?"

"Not yet. I'm still learning."

"Then join me for coffee and I'll explain why I'm protesting."

"Okay." I had nothing better to do. The museum could wait.

I followed him. We walked to the roundabout and then took a side street. After a minute we randomly happened upon a small café. We entered and took seats at the bar and ordered doppios.

To my surprise Jan bought the woman next to him a

macchiato. She was short, with teak-colored hair and bright white teeth. He then turned his attention to a short list of specials advertised on a green chalkboard hung behind the bar. He said maybe he would come back later for lunch.

He then ignored me and started wooing the woman. I didn't blame him; she was cute. They eventually exchanged names and phone numbers. Only then did he turn his attention back to me. "I'll meet her for lunch." He smiled. "Or maybe dinner."

And then he started in about CRISPR. "It's not an easy issue."

"So, what are your concerns?" I asked. "You're a scientist, so what's the problem? Why are you protesting?"

He reached into his shoulder bag and handed me a brochure.

I should have known.

He saw my skepticism. "No. It's not another self-referential propaganda brochure." He smiled. "That's not my style. I'm not cannon fodder for someone else's protest. It's not just another generic brochure, either. I know what it's like to go to a website and find the same repetitive message, just packaged a dozen different ways. All pushing the same propaganda. What you have in your hands is *my* brochure, with *my* concerns, *my* reasoning, and all in *my* own words."

Yep. Sounds like a guy with three PhDs. I opened the brochure and saw his name, Jan Larsen, under the catchy title *Off-target Mutations*.

He added, "But it's what you have to do. Changing someone's mind is a Sisyphean task."

My hand wrapped around my phone. I wanted to say, "Aletheia, please define Sisyphean," but I restrained myself.

"Some protesters are worried about designer babies. And eugenics. Others are worried about harming nature, or they object to how animals are treated in genetic experiments. Those are legitimate concerns. My main concern, though, is the potential for an accident. I am concerned that a scientist will edit the wrong genes. It's called an off-target mutation. And it can be tragic. An off-target mutation can cause a really bad, unintended birth defect."

"So this means you're against using human embryos?" I felt proud of myself. I had learned enough about CRISPR to have a basic discussion. I guess I owed that to Dr. Keyes and our conversation last night.

"Yes. Unfortunately, scientists are already using human embryos. And they have injected human stem cells into pig embryos, creating a part-pig, part-human embryo. Private money is funding their research. I just want genetic engineering to be transparent so everyone knows what is happening. And regulated the best we can."

He continued. "We have a choice: either regulation and transparency, or tragic, unintended consequences. That's my concern. Off-target mutations."

I said, "I heard that scientists are modifying organisms or even creating new organisms, and then applying for patents? That concerns me. Do companies or people have the right to own genetically engineered life?"

"I'm concerned about that, too." He smiled. "Liko, you're welcome to join our protest."

"Thanks, but I still have a lot to learn before I take sides."

We left the café. I walked with him to the street corner, where we both stopped. We turned and faced each other. It was time to part: Jan back to the protest line, me to the Bargello.

"You can always join our protest," he offered again.

I doubted that. I had never been in a protest. I DO believe in open debate, though. I believe people must sit down, talk and discuss facts, ideas, and personal concerns. Just like Jan and I did. Both sides must listen. We must not cover our ears and dig in our heels. I loathe people who lock in their positions, like those white evangelical pro-testers. I'm glad I listened to Jan. Learned his concerns. I hoped that the scientists at the conference would listen, too.

"Why did you follow me out of the hotel?"

He stared at me a long moment. "I was interested in the woman at your table."

"What about her?"

"Istina used to be my girlfriend."

My eyes must have enlarged and my mouth must have dropped open, because he laughed, and then he smiled. It was a friendly smile. "But I think that you know noth-ing. You are . . ." A longer pause. "Be careful." The light changed and he started across the street.

I was furious to get the warning with no other informa-tion. As he walked away I said in a loud voice, "So why is someone trying to kill her?"

He spun around. Concern instantly replaced his happy-go-lucky countenance.

"I'm going to the Bargello. Join me." I turned abruptly and marched off down the sidewalk in the direction of the museum. As I expected, he was right behind me. He caught up at the next corner, coming up beside me.

"We should share what we know," I suggested, although I really had no idea what I was talking about.

"Okay," he said. "What happened? Someone tried to kill Istina?"

I smiled. This was the only success I'd had in the last four days! This was Istina's former boyfriend! I expected answers soon. Hallelujah!

But then Istina's advice to me suddenly became relevant. No one knew who I was. No one knew that I had killed a man in Rome. No one could connect me to Istina and her brother and the dead man. So what could I safely tell Jan? What could I tell Jan without compromising my own identity and safety?

So, I focused on Istina. I started with her identity. "What is Istina's research all about?"

"She started as an undergraduate at Harvard. That is where she first studied the human genome. During her senior year she became interested in the human microbiome, and how our bodies are hosts to microorganisms. She graduated with honors in genetics. She then returned home to Saudi Arabia."

"She was born in Saudi Arabia?"

"Yes."

"And her brother, too?"

"Faisal? Yes."

"Do you know why anyone would want to hurt Faisal?"

"No."

"So she left school and moved back home to Saudi Arabia. Did she move in with her parents?"

"No." Jan cleared his throat. "Well, I don't know where she lived in Saudi Arabia. But that's where she met Dr. Charmchi. Dr. Charmchi was working in amphibians and reptiles and how they regenerated their body parts. Regeneration became Istina's new passion. She took a year off to read and learn everything available on regeneration."

"She took a year off from what?"

"School." Jan looked at me kind of funny.

"And then she went back to school?"

"Yes. She returned to the States and pursued her graduate studies at Stanford University. That's where I met her, we worked together in the same lab. We mapped the genes of a large salamander. We also learned how the genes triggered and controlled the rate of tissue regeneration." Jan smiled. "For that we both received our Masters in Science."

I was impressed. I had never been in a real lab.

Jan continued. "She then did original PhD work on genetic mechanisms—how to control the rate of tissue and organ regeneration in reptiles and amphibians. She worked first at the University of California-Berkeley and then the University of North Carolina at Chapel Hill. That's when we lost touch. We lived together in Berkeley, but I didn't follow her to Carolina. My research kept me in California."

"Is that where she got her patent?"

"At Carolina? No. Her patents came later. But she earned her reputation at UNC."

"What did she do there?"

"Mammalian regeneration. She then conducted postdoctoral research into mammalian regeneration at Sun Yat-Sen University, in China. Her team established parallels between the genes in amphibians and reptiles that control regeneration and similar, vestigial genes in mammals, including people. Her team made several breakthroughs, which led to a flood of funding to pursue both her team and individual interests."

"And what is she doing now?"

"Last year she received a grant, which she took with her when she left Sun Yat-Sen University. That upset a lot of researchers there."

A possible motive, I thought. "But that didn't stop her?"

"No. She started independent research in transgenics aboard *The Veritas*, a state-of-the-art research vessel kept in international waters."

"And now, here?"

"She is at the conference seeking additional funds."

"By herself?"

"Oh, no. You were with them at breakfast. Dr. Keyes and Dr. Crisp. Those are their nicknames, anyway."

"What is the name of the guy who wears the fancy Armani suits and is always hanging around her?"

"He's an investor, not a scientist. I don't remember his name."

"I call him The Suit."

"Okay."

"And the guy in the designer sunglasses?"

"Dr. Crisp. Let me compliment you again on your sunglasses. They look nice."

"They're Prada."

"Expensive?"

"No, I got them cheap."

We both smiled. I chuckled, thinking how smoothly that scene had played out. It could have been loud and messy. And bloody—at least his nose, anyway.

"Dr. Crisp is an unethical asshole. No one likes him."

"He seems close to Istina."

Jan flinched. "I answered your questions, so answer mine: why do you think someone is trying to hurt Istina?"

Perhaps I should have hesitated, made up an answer, told only part of the truth, but I'm honest to the core. "Istina and her brother were attacked at a metro station in Rome. I saw it. Three men in business suits attacked them. I was there. I stopped them. One of the men is dead, killed with his own knife. The other two: one ran after Istina's brother, the other ran off after I . . . the stabbing."

He pursed his lips. "What did they look like?"

"Dark gray suits. Early thirties, maybe."

"Besides the suits? Anything unique? Different?"

"Not that I remember. They had foreign accents, though. Like Leonardo DiCaprio in *Blood Diamonds*. Did you see that film?"

"A South African accent?"

"Is that what it is? One of them yelled something like 'fok jou' at me as he backed off. He was white, not black. I thought maybe German, but that didn't quite fit."

"Afrikaans. Afrikaners have an unusual accent." He smiled. "'Dit sou beslis uit plek wees in Italie.'"

"Yeah, that's it." I smiled.

"I lived there a while. My undergraduate work was in organismal biology. I collected amphibians and reptiles in South Africa's national parks."

I smiled again. I was pleased that he was interested in biology, like me. "I don't think the attack was random. So they may be looking for Istina and her brother."

"Istina is easy to find. Everyone knows she's attending the conference. She has a major presentation today. I was going to slip in to listen to it, but I saw you at her table . . . and here I am instead."

"Could the men be after her brother, not her?" I asked.

He thought for a moment. "I have no idea? I don't even know what Faisal does these days. And I have no idea where he is or how to find him."

We walked a block together, thinking.

He broke the silence: "If they are after her brother, not her, they may already be here, watching her, waiting, hoping that her brother will show up or that she will lead them to him."

We arrived at the Bargello. "I need to get back," he said. We shook hands. He said, "Keep on the lookout for gray suits speaking Afrikaans."

I nodded agreement.

And then he left.

I spent the rest of the day at the Museo Nazionale del Bargello, hoping that Istina would join me. All day long, as I wondered past masterpieces by Donatello and Michelangelo, thoughts of her invaded my mind and I recalled moments from dinner last night.

Outside and inside the museum, people clustered. I overheard gossip about family and friends, some of it nasty. Somebody wronged somebody. A woman and man chattered back and forth. No genius clusters here.

My thoughts turned inward. What did people say about me when they gossiped? Unlike Jan and Istina, I had barely graduated from high school. And I was culturally unrefined, having grown up in a trailer park. I was so large that people seldom saw past the physical me. They saw I was tall, almost 6 feet 3 inches; muscular, almost 250 pounds with a broad chest and shoulders; slightly uncoordinated—a bit clumsy at times but I'm growing out of that; rich olive-brown skin, now that I spend time outdoors; a somewhat flattened yet arched nose; large black eyes and long black lashes; and wavy black hair. Like Istina, my lips were thick, turned outward and, I think, voluptuous. Her full lips are voluptuous, and they are like mine.

I soon found myself on the ground floor in the courtyard, or what the museum brochure labeled the *piano terra*.

I was standing in front of the crouching statue of *The Fisher Boy and Oceano*. It reminded me of little Ned, the grandson of an old Japanese fisherman I knew in Oahu. Ned was only four or five years old when I met him. I had watched the old fisherman show little Ned how to skin an eel that was half as long as the boy.

I took the wide stairway to the first floor and entered the Donatello room. And there stood Donatello's *David*, sculpted in 1440! There were too many tourists in the room, all chattering away, so I plugged in my earbuds and raised the volume of my music.

I felt rapture. I had expected to feel this way when I stepped into the Duomo yesterday, but instead I experienced it here at the feet of Donatello's vision of David. His *David* was nude between his laurel-topped hat and knee-high boots. Uncircumcised, yet effeminate.

David's left boot rested upon the head of Goliath. The giant's beard wrapped the boot, partially. The long, lush feathers of a wing on top of Goliath's helmet caressed the inside of David's thigh, from his boot to his crotch. Hot! I gazed at *David*.

At this moment, I have no doubt that Donatello was homosexual and that his *David* was gay. My Uncle Keahi, who is also gay, would love this!

And then I discovered in the same room a cherubic *Statue of Love*, also by Donatello. I fell in love with the little statue. I tried taking a picture with my phone but I couldn't get the lighting right.

I climbed to the armory on the second floor, or as it was labeled in the museum guide, "Secondo Piano – armoury." The armory hall included a child's suit of armor. I found that deeply disturbing.

Did I want to be a soldier, a mercenary, or a warrior? No!

Yet I would describe myself as a protector, a guardian, and a defender.

Before I left my hotel this morning, I had asked the concierge where I might find a nice gift for a woman. I wasn't sure why, but I thought it might be helpful if I gave Istina a gift. I guess I didn't know what else to do, and I was willing to try anything that might work.

I now pulled the piece of paper out of my pocket, unfolded it, and read her handwriting: Officina Profumo Farmaceutica, Di Santa Maria Novella SPA, Via della Scala, 16, 50123 Firenze. I found my way to the nearest taxi-cab stand and soon arrived at the perfume shop.

For my great-aunt I purchased Sapone Latte Rosa. For Keahi, 100 grams of Te' Fiori E Frutta sacc. And for Istina: an intoxicating perfume. I also bought a tube of Crema Pedestre; as soon as I saw the tube, I fantasized about giving some future girlfriend a foot massage. I had never given anyone a foot massage. After massaging my imaginary girlfriend's feet, I imagined rubbing her calves and the inside of her thighs. So I bought some perfumed body butter, too, just in case. I'd be optimistic.

I returned to my hotel and put the presents next to the writing table in my room. I then changed into my Canali suit for my return to the Grand Hotel. I was hopeful that Jan had had some luck with Istina.

I also wondered if the protestors would still be there. If so, then they would have put in a hard day. I half imagined that I'd see the young woman Jan had met in the café. I imagined her protesting with him now.

But I dressed in my fine Canali suit, and that was my passport. I expected to cross the line of protesters and to enter the hotel without any problems. No one would question me. The policewoman and policeman from this morning would probably be gone. If the protestors were still there, a new shift would be on duty. No one would recognize me, no one would stop me. I would just walk freely through the hotel entrance.

But when I arrived I saw an ambulance in front of the Grand Hotel. It was a boxy van with AMBULANZA in bright orange letters across the slanted front of the van and the driver area. The blue lights flashed, highlighting horizontal yellow and orange stripes. I could see Fratellanza Militare Firenze in black letters on the side and front of the van, too. The ambulance pulled away as I approached.

The protestors had gone home for the day. I noticed several posters strewn on the ground. A few were broken. And then I saw a ragtag group of protestors off to the side of the square, next to the Arno River. The police kept them off the square and a good distance from the Grand Hotel. The American protestors were gone, and Jan was not in sight, either.

I asked the doorman, "What happened?"

"A protestor got stabbed."

"Is he okay?"

"They are taking him to the hospital."

"That's too bad," I said.

A sudden recognition flashed on the doorman's face. "I saw the two of you together this morning. The two of you left the hotel together."

"Jan?" I said. "Was his name Jan Larsen? What did he look like?" I described Jan.

The doorman's attitude changed. Grown suspicious? I was glad that I had worn the suit this time.

"Yes, I met him earlier today," I said, telling the truth. I always tell the truth. I still don't know if that is a weakness or strength. "Was anyone else hurt?"

"Not that I am aware of, sir. But whoever did this got away. They did not catch him."

Just great, I thought.

He must have seen the concern cross my face for his attitude changed again. The doorman no longer held me in suspicion. I was now a worried guest. "The polizia have everything in control."

"Of course," I said. Of course, the police didn't know squat. "Where did they take him? Which hospital?"

"Careggi. The best in the city, sir."

"Good," I said. "That's good."

Istina was not in the lobby or at the bar. Neither was Dr. Keyes or anyone else from her team. I checked the concurrent sessions; as I suspected, they had already ended for the day. But there was a poster session advertised in one of the ballrooms. It started at 5:30pm, so perhaps she would be there. Or if not, maybe someone else could tell me her whereabouts.

I wandered up and down stairways and hallways until I finally stumbled upon the ballroom. I entered and perused the posters on easels along the four walls. The poster topics were catchy: robotic arms out of animal muscle tissue, cameras out of eye cells, and olfactory sensors from the nasal cells of basset hounds.

Occasionally there was a booth offering brochures, cheap giveaways, and videos. I opened a brochure and read what looked like a reprinted newspaper headline: "Innovative synthetic biology company seeks venture capital." It was a cleverly disguised request for funding.

I stepped out of the booth and surveyed the room again. A few people were milling about but I did not see Istina.

I boldly stopped by the front desk and had the woman call Istina's room. No answer. And then Dr. Keyes' room; again, no answer. I left a message with my name and cell phone number: "Please give me a call, I need to talk to you. It is urgent."

I called Careggi Hospital but they refused to release information about Jan, other than to say that he was alive. Visitors were allowed, but only during the daytime, and with picture identification. That obviously wouldn't work. But neither could I sneak into the hospital and find my way to his room: I didn't know Italian, so I couldn't read signs and follow directions to his room by myself. Besides, he might be in surgery, medicated, or asleep. And the woman on the phone wouldn't even give me his room number!

I had no doubt that one of the men in gray suits had stabbed him. Had their Afrikaans accent given them away? I also felt sure that the men in gray suits were long gone. They wouldn't be hanging around tonight, but they'd be back. Istina was their target, not Jan.

Frustration overwhelmed me. I had failed the girl in the quarry. Had I failed Jan, too? Hadn't I? But I wouldn't fail Istina.

I found my way back to the hotel bar and sat at a small, round table in a corner. I ordered a bottle of wine and drank it on ice cubes, a bad preference of mine. But I like my wine cold.

For a few minutes I focused on the few conversations in the bar. No Afrikaans. I looked around. Almost everyone was in a suit. Hell! Even I was in a suit. I took off my tie and draped it over the back of the chair opposite me. It was too

warm for a tie. Besides, I'm sure that ties aggravate claustrophobia, so why would I, of all people, want to wear one?

My attention turned back to Istina. I checked my phone.
She and Dr. Keyes had not returned my call. I set my
iPhone face up next to my glass of red wine.

Taking a deep breath, I assessed how I felt physically
and mentally. I was tired, on edge, hot, pissed, and I had
had too much to drink. I gulped down the last swallows of
wine in my glass, and then pushed the almost empty bottle
away from me, to the opposite side of the table. I sighed.

The wine encouraged my mind to wander and I was
soon thinking about Jan's relationship with Istina. So Jan
had been her boyfriend. That made sense. They were
about the same age. He seemed brilliant, like her. He was
handsome, she was beautiful. They probably got excited
spending long hours in the laboratory studying genes and
genomes and other 'small things.' I'm not like that. We had
different scale views of the world. I like the ocean. DNA
fascinates them.

I admitted to myself that I was lonely. During my adventure I had been hoping for someone to suddenly appear,
to be my friend, lover, soul mate. I thought about Istina
and Jan. They had found each other and been a couple. I
imagined that Istina's next boyfriend would be sedentary,
bookish, a laboratory geek: a number-crunching, statisti-
cian-type who loved chemistry, physics, and computing.
Like one of the guys at the conference, but NOT me. I
wanted a girlfriend to travel the world with: a tomboy, not
a scientist.

Was Istina's research a force for good or evil in the
world? I picked up my phone and Googled it. There were
a lot of photographs of her and I clicked quickly through
them. A few pictures of her and Dr. Keyes and other col-

leagues. A picture of her in a white lab coat in a laboratory. A romantic picture of her and Jan at a beach somewhere.

Then I found her bio and picture on a Sun Yat-Sen University web page from a presentation she gave last year. Also a photo of her in a dark auditorium, packed with professionally dressed people. She was pointing at an embryo—I didn't know the species, but it was not human—on a movie-theater-sized screen behind her. She looked confident. Her dress fit her perfectly.

I was reading a blog article about her when my phone rang: Dr. Keyes.

"What do you want?" he asked. "I am sure that Istina is already in bed."

Did he think that I was pining for Istina? I smiled. Perhaps that is the only reason he would have returned my call. He thinks I have a crush—a hopeless crush—on Istina. Dr. Keyes must be a romantic at heart. I had to smile at that.

I said, "I'm calling with some bad news."

I waited for his acknowledgement.

"What?"

"Do you know a researcher named Jan Larsen?"

There was silence on the phone and for a moment I thought that I had just lost Dr. Keyes. I had no idea what his relationship with Jan was. Maybe I had made another major faux pas?

"Yes," came his hesitant reply.

"I met him today. He has been outside the hotel, protesting. Did you know that?"

"No."

"He said he used to be Istina's boyfriend."

"I see. You're interested in her former boyfriends now? You are a sad case."

I almost smiled at his faulty conclusion. "No. No. Jan was stabbed outside the hotel this evening."

After another period of silence, he said, "Is he okay?"

"I don't know. They took him to the local hospital."

"I see."

"I need to see Istina before she leaves."

Silence again.

"Can you help me?"

Silence.

"It's important. Very important."

"We'll meet you at breakfast at the usual time."

"Around seven o' clock?"

"Yes. That works. Our shuttle doesn't leave until noon for the airport."

"Thank you," I said. "It IS very important."

This was great news! I returned to my own hotel and went to bed. I'd see them tomorrow at breakfast. I'd finally get some answers. Yet I didn't sleep well.

6

I sat at a table in the Winter Garden restaurant near the buffet, facing a man carving thin slices of prime rib and a woman making omelets and crepes to order. I positioned my chair to face the baked goods: croissants, baguettes, cheeses, marmalades and other spreads. The position also gave me a view of the dining area.

After ordering cappuccino and the buffet, I filled my plate and ate slowly, waiting for Istina or someone, anyone, from her team to arrive.

I knew my return to the restaurant was reckless. The man in the round sunglasses had warned me twice, and I had taken his sunglasses. Being here was definitely poor judgment.

But when I awoke this morning I could think of nothing but Istina and our meeting. I even woke up during the night. The events of Rome kept replaying again and again.

I took inventory of myself: my thoughts, my feelings, my physical body—all were focused completely on Istina. Today I would solve the mystery of why a man was dead in Rome and why someone had stabbed Jan. At any moment, anything could happen. I had never been this alive, this aware, this much in the moment, in my entire life. I felt as if my body were supercharged. It felt great!

I had a croissant. An orange juice. I was hungry, yet I was not interested in relieving my hunger. I sipped my cappuccino but I was already wide awake.

A few minutes after 7:30am, when Istina hadn't appeared, I began to worry. Had I missed her? My calm outward composure evaporated as my eyes surveyed the room, table by table. I paid my bill and left the restaurant.

As I approached the man at the hotel registration desk, I felt anxious and a bit fearful, not of the man at the desk, but generally weak because I anticipated the answer he might give me. I gathered my courage to ask about Istina and Dr. Keyes, and I received the reply I dreaded to hear: "She left, sir."

And with that she was gone. I'd lost her. I hadn't gotten her phone number or email. Fuck! I thought I had more time. Fuck! There was never enough time.

"Do you have her phone number? Email address?"

"Sorry, sir, we can't give out that information."

Dr. Keyes had said they would leave for the airport at noon, but he lied. He obviously booked an earlier shuttle bus. He had deceived me. They must have left for the airport before I even arrived for breakfast!

Was he involved in the attack on Istina and her brother, I wondered? Or was it someone else at the conference? Now I would never know.

I didn't even have the interest or energy now to walk across the lobby and leave the hotel, so I dropped into a lounge chair near the reservation desk. I didn't care what the men at the desk and the bellhop thought.

So much for protecting her, I thought. And I would never know who was trying to hurt her, and why.

And then my mind returned once again to the terrible events of the young woman drowning in the flooded quarry, almost two years ago. I had failed her, too. There was a pattern of failure. I foolishly snorkeled at Hanauma Bay before I could swim, and as a result, Angelica—a close friend of Uncle Keahi's—almost drowned. Later that summer I foolishly scuba dived with Uncle Keahi in an attempt to earn my advanced diving certificate. We both could have drowned because I was swept away by a strong current and it was nighttime. Both times Uncle rescued me. The following year, I let my emotions cloud my judgment when I demanded permission to dive the caves at Shark's Cove in Hawaii. Fortunately Uncle Keahi refused permission. My would-have-been dive partner drowned. Even after that event I was too proud to admit my responsibility. Instead, I was offended that Uncle Keahi did not allow me to dive. I held him responsible for the diver's death.

And I failed once again. I was suddenly tired. I placed the paper sack containing my gift to Istina on the coffee table, closed my eyes, and fell asleep.

At first I thought I was dreaming. But when I reached for her hand, it was real: warm and soft, but larger than I had expected. Istina had awakened me.

Before I fully awoke, I gave her the brown sack with her gift inside.

"What's this?" She held the paper sack but did not open it.

"A gift for you."

"Thank you," she said.

I noticed immediately that she was not happy. She wasn't smiling. She was preoccupied; her eyes glanced around the lobby, searching, questioning, and anxious.

Curious, I scanned the lobby, too, but I saw nothing unusual. I was surprised, though, that no one had disturbed me while I slept. How long had I been out? An hour? Two?

"Come with me," she directed curtly. With that she took me by the hand and led me out to the first taxi, waiting.

I followed willingly. I noticed that my knees were a bit weak and wobbly. Was it because I had just awakened and the blood had rushed to my head, or was it because she had taken me by the hand?

"Where are we going?" I asked.

"Siena."

"Okay. Sure." I didn't know what direction Siena was in or how far a drive it was; I was just happy to be with her, even though she had captured me instead of me capturing her. I had one more chance to get answers. My pulse quickened.

We sat close to each other in the back seat of the Fiat, her small brown leather purse resting in the narrow space between us. I had a good view of the driver. I could see the upper half of his face, including his eyes, in the rearview mirror.

Istina and I said nothing at first. We were both anxious. She glanced again and again out the taxi windows, both sides and behind us. I glanced at her occasionally, nervous yet happy to be sitting next to her. I wasn't sure how to behave, what to say, what to do. Sitting next to her, my mind reeled.

"I saw one of them," she said.

"Where?" I glanced out her window and then mine. The road was climbing fast and steep, but no one was out there. I looked out the rear window. A small white car was following us, but it was a young couple—the girl sitting close to a boy driver—nothing to be concerned about. I was happy for them.

"One of the men was waiting for me. He knew my airline, Brussels Airlines."

"You were flying to Brussels?"

"First Brussels, then Iceland."

I tried to imagine Iceland, a place I had never been: a frozen island, blonde-haired white people in puffy winter coats, snow and ice. I guessed that *The Veritas* was somewhere near Iceland. That must have been Istina's final destination.

"And where is Dr. Keyes?" I asked.

Istina placed a hand on my forearm. "I left him at the airport." She laughed fretfully. "When Dr. Keyes stepped out of the taxi, I saw one of the men waiting for me, the man from the Rome metro. Fortunately I saw him first." She squeezed my forearm.

"Damn! What happened?"

"I told the taxi driver, 'I forgot my coat – my magenta coat.' Dr. Keyes knows I am fond of it."

I'm fond of it too, I thought.

"The taxi driver said we had time to drive back to the hotel and return to the airport, given that our flight didn't leave for another hour and a half. So I told him, 'Make the round trip, let's do it.'"

"But it's at least four to five hours from Florence to Rome, isn't it?"

"Yes, but I was flying from Vespucci airport here in Florence, not Rome."

"I see."

"Dr. Keyes was furious. He said the hotel could mail me the coat. He said we'd miss the flight. We'd have to spend another night in Florence. He was *not* happy, but I insisted. I told him, 'You stay here and check in. If I don't return in time, leave without me. Don't wait for me. I'll catch the next flight.'"

I nodded.

"Dr. Keyes argued, but the taxi driver and I left. It is amazing how fast he drove, but he was game for it." She shook her head sadly. "But poor Dr. Keyes . . ."

"Did the man see you?"

"No, but I'm sure he saw Dr. Keyes when he dropped off his suitcase curbside. Maybe he followed him into the airport, I don't know. He was probably wondering where I was. Probably still waiting for me to show up, too."

"Just one man?"

"Yes, just one. The man who sprinted up the escalator after my brother."

I replayed the memory: the man had stepped on Istina and then raced up the down escalator. That time, I wasn't close enough to help her, to stop him, but I wouldn't let it happen again.

I said, "Jan thought the man had an Afrikaans accent."

"Jan who?"

"Jan Larsen."

I watched her face. Jan's name didn't register.

"Your former boyfriend?"

Her eyes questioned me. Suddenly she let go of my forearm and sat up straight. Her loose, whimsical braids shifted, resettled on her shoulders, and cascaded onto the front of her beige blouse. I glanced at the colorful highlights in one of the braids and found my favorite color: orange.

"Didn't Dr. Keyes tell you?"

"No." My gaze returned to her face. She now looked puzzled, concerned. "Tell me what?"

"I called Dr. Keyes last night. I told him about Jan."

I tried to read her face. She was trying to understand, trying to fit her former boyfriend into the current situation, but she was genuinely bewildered.

"Jan Larsen, he was stabbed yesterday."

"Stabbed?" She inhaled sharply and covered her mouth with both hands.

"He was ambulanced to the hospital.

"Is he okay?"

"I called but they wouldn't give me any information. And I couldn't visit, obviously."

"I have to see him." Her left hand grabbed the armrest on the taxi door. Her other hand grabbed my forearm again. I thought she was going to lean forward and command the taxi driver to turn around, immediately, and drive back to Florence and the hospital.

"Probably not a good idea." I glanced at the taxi driver to see if he was listening. He seemed oblivious. Nevertheless I resolved to tip him generously.

I glanced back at Istina. She was looking at me, yet her hazel eyes were elsewhere. And then she blinked, refocused on me, and said, "You're right. It's not a good idea. They may be watching the hospital, too."

I thought she was going to cry. Until that moment she had seemed in control, completely. Strong and formidable. I liked that strength. I liked it a lot. I was saddened to see it breached.

"I met him yesterday on my way to the Bargello. He was

in front of the hotel with the protestors." My comment surprised and upset her. Was she still fond of Jan? Or was his protest a betrayal? I had no idea. "I told him about the attack in Rome, about the three men."

"What?" she snapped. "And the man you killed?"

"More or less. Kind of."

"Why did you do that?"

I shrugged my shoulders.

"How could you be so stupid?" She pulled away from me. Her body pressed against the door on her side of the taxi.

"I don't understand," I said.

"He was probably attacked because of you."

Her accusation startled me. I glanced to see if the taxi driver had heard. His eyes were still on the road. I looked back quickly at Istina.

"Liko, he wasn't involved. Damn you! I told you to leave, to disappear. Why didn't you?" She was royally pissed. "Instead you brought him into it."

"Yes, because you refused to talk to me. I know you're mad. But I'm not 'disappearing' until I have answers." I wanted to add, *Because I killed a man to save your life,* but I controlled myself.

"Liko, I know Jan. He probably walked around, talked to everybody, listened to their accents." She sighed. "He found somebody, obviously."

Some of the beauty drained from her face. Her eyes changed too; what was it that I saw? Her eyes were now less green, more amber—her pupils darker. The change was unnerving. I didn't like it.

I glanced again in the rearview mirror. The driver was still watching the road. He might be listening, but he wasn't watching us.

"So what did you tell him?" she demanded.

"I told Jan that the men had an unusual accent: kind of German, but not. Jan thought they might be from South Africa, Afrikaners."

She mulled over my comment and then frowned. Wrinkles appeared above her eyebrows where they furrowed together. The green had vanished completely from her hazel eyes, leaving dark amber pupils at the center of orange flares. A little scary, but beautiful.

An idea came to me: maybe they were professionals, perhaps bounty hunters. I recalled a Hawaii-based TV show I used to watch called *Dog the Bounty Hunter*. Dog was laid-back and didn't wear a suit, though. Street smart. Muscular. I met him and his wife in person once at a Red Lobster restaurant in Waikiki. He seemed like a nice guy, I liked him. *No*, I concluded, *I doubt that the men in suits were bounty hunters.*

And then I had another idea, but this time I said it aloud: "Maybe they're assassins? Professionals?"

Istina stared at me. Her hands balled into fists. Was she going to hit me? She seemed really pissed, but I couldn't think what I had done wrong.

She stared me in the eyes and nodded her head, slowly. The nod said it all: *Yes, they are professionals.* And then she tilted her head towards the taxi driver. It was a warning. She said, in a low voice, "I'll tell you later."

I nodded agreement.

By the time we entered Chianti she had calmed down, at least a little bit. Perhaps it was the green hills and the vineyards and the olive trees and the stone buildings. Or perhaps we were both exhausted and needed to 'recharge our batteries,' so to speak.

I checked the sun and determined we were heading south. "How far is it to Siena?" I asked.

"Fifty-nine miles from Florence," the drive volunteered. "Another thirty minutes."

Great! I thought. *The driver HAS been listening.* I'd have to tip him very generously.

Minutes later, I watched Istina open the small sack and remove the perfume and then the foot cream. Seeing the foot cream, I blushed. I had not meant to give her that. It was meant for my future girlfriend, my imaginary girl-friend who, so far, was just air-built.

"Thank you." She dabbed perfume on her wrists and rubbed them together. "Wonderful." She then read the backside of the foot cream tube. "I need to walk more. Get more exercise." She smiled and said, "Thank you."

The green had returned to her hazel eyes, and with it, beauty once again filled her face. I couldn't help but focus on her mouth as she smiled.

So my present had provided a momentary distraction, a temporary consolation. It had become a peace offering. That made me feel better.

Sitting this close to her, I could see that she was at least fifteen, maybe twenty years older than me. She had to be in her late thirties. Was that a problem?

A problem for what? The attraction I was beginning to feel for her? I was a bit surprised, still . . . it was all nat-ural, wasn't it? As natural as her beautiful braids, her fiery eyes, her slender body seated just inches from me. I didn't care about our age difference. I hoped that she didn't care, either.

Perhaps it was the high humidity, but I could smell not

only the perfume, but also Istina. It was not sweet like sugar or an aphrodisiac like licorice, but it was salty. Her body odor, the smell of her hair, they both reminded me of the ocean. I liked that.

When we arrived in Siena, I gave the taxi driver an overly generous tip. I asked for his name, and he gave me his card. I thanked him profusely and then gave him an additional tip.

As we stepped out of the taxi it began to rain.

"Where is your luggage?" I asked, hoping to retrieve her magenta coat from a suitcase in the trunk of the taxi.

"I ditched it at the hotel. Left it with the doorman."

"You're not going back to the hotel, I hope."

She thought for a moment. "I'll have them send the luggage to wherever we stay tonight."

'Wherever we stay tonight?' That startled me. "Or just abandon it," I said. "That's what I'd do."

The temperature dropped several degrees, quickly. Wet and now cold, we shivered.

We ducked into a tourist gift shop and considered buying either a bright yellow or dull purple umbrella. They were the only ones left. Istina chose a bright yellow. We tried on inexpensive jackets for warmth, and selected one light blue and one dark blue, with matching ITALIA in large white letters across the front.

Istina had worn open-toed sandals, so her feet were now wet and cold. I watched patiently as she tried on shoes at a small, neighboring store. She selected a pair of brightly colored Italian running shoes.

She stood in front of me, happy in her bright pink patterned shoes, light blue jacket with white ITALIA in large letters across her chest, and holding a bright yellow umbrella. I smiled and laughed, happy too.

It was still raining and cold, so we stopped at a café for tea. I had a doppio. She introduced me to my first pan-forte, delicious. I read the ingredients: candied orange and citron, almonds, sugar, hazelnuts, honey, cinnamon, nutmeg, vanilla. From inside her warm jacket and comfortable shoes, she smiled.

We finally reached the fan-shaped Piazza del Campo, well known for the Palio di Siena horse races twice each year. In front of us were great palaces, civic palaces. From the bricked plaza it was uphill in almost every direction. I gazed happily at hilltops.

From the Piazzo del Campo, we strolled together to the Piazzo of the Duomo and the largest church in Siena. She held my arm and I held the bright yellow umbrella against the drizzle. Occasionally our bodies pressed against each other. I liked that.

Before entering the massive Gothic structure, we stopped to gaze at a statue of a wolf with two small boys crouching beneath her for protection. According to legend, one of the small boys was Remus, whose sons founded Siena. The statue was reputed to be stolen from the Temple of Apollo, in Rome.

We entered the Duomo and I was overwhelmed. A lot of Goth. Columns layered and striped dramatically. White marble inlaid with stripes of dark greenish-black marble. It was the kind of décor I would expect in a pagan temple. But then I realized that a lot of what I'd seen in the last few days was recycled, including statues and gold and even marble. Stuff looted or pillaged or stolen during Crusades or other military campaigns. One empire falls. Another rises. Only now were these museums and churches frozen in time—at least for the moment it appeared so.

The brochure I was reading noted that there were 36

heads of emperors and 102 heads of popes surrounding us, high overhead in long rows. They all looked alike to me. Only the names inscribed below them were different, yet in a very boring way.

We progressed up the aisle. According to the brochure, the floor was normally covered by a carpet, but it was our good fortune to arrive during the feast of one of Siena's saints.

I spotted the she-wolf again, but this time in marble mosaic on the floor, nursing her twins. I pointed it out to Istina. According to our brochure, these twins were the sons of Remus. They had fled to escape the wrath of their uncle Romulus.

"She's more coyote than wolf," I said, trying to impress Istina. I didn't know anything about the Roman myth, but I knew about dogs, wolves, and coyotes. Like most boys growing up in America—even in a trailer park outside Las Vegas—I'd read Jack London's *Call of the Wild*. And I'd seen pictures of gray wolves. This was not a gray wolf.

"Really? How so?"

"The long pointed ears, the narrow pointed snout, the long, lean torso. That's a coyote."

"So wolves have rounded ears? Blunt snouts? Are bigger and heavier?"

"Gray wolves are."

"Maybe Eurasian wolves are different?"

Goodness, I thought. *She was probably right. The she-wolf would be a European species, not North American.* I felt deflated.

She must have realized that my pride was at stake because she didn't pursue it.

Instead we stood next to each other, staring at the she-wolf. Her large head hung below her chest, watchful of the twins. One firmly grasped a tit, greedily sucking, and the other crouched alert. Both were muscular, filled out. Super babies.

Istina pointed at a raised paw. "Look at those sharp yellow nails."

"Canines walk on their nails," I explained.

"Even on marble?" she countered with a smile.

Was she joking, or questioning me again? I wasn't sure. Nevertheless, I now found myself wondering if wolves could retract their nails. Could they? On a smooth surface, like marble, would they retract their nails and walk on their padded paws? I didn't know for sure, so I said, "They tap dance. On marble they tap dance."

She smiled. I smiled. And we both laughed.

I almost said 'their nails are to marble like our fingernails are to chalkboards,' but that was over the top so I kept quiet.

We then encountered another story on the floor: the massacre of the innocents. Soldiers were forcing babies from the arms of their mothers and then murdering them with swords and daggers. A dagger was plunged into the chest of one baby, and another soldier held an infant, impaled on a long dagger, over the heads of two women who frantically clutched another child to their chests. The white marble body of an impaled infant contrasted with the black marble background. I found it nauseating. Dead babies lay lifeless at the feet of the soldiers.

"Who imagined such an atrocity?" Istina asked, shaking her head.

"I can ask Aletheia," I pulled my iPhone out of my front jeans pocket and turned on her app.

"Istina, please meet Aletheia. She is my personal scholar."

Istina raised an eyebrow.

"Aletheia, please meet Istina. She is the Queen of Genetics." I snapped a picture of Istina. I knew that Aletheia would access it in the Photo app.

"Pleased to meet you Istina," Aletheia stated. There was artificial pleasure in her voice. She then volunteered, "I have read all of your scientific papers and everything else about you on the web. I digested and summarized everything for Liko in five hundred words or less."

"That's terrible!" Istina blurted out. "Everything about me in five hundred words?"

"Yes," Aletheia volunteered, thinking that Istina had asked her the question. "Liko instructed 'summarize in five hundred words or less.' I summarized in four hundred ninety three."

"That's embarrassing," I said, blushing. "A little too much information, there, Aletheia."

"You are welcome, Liko. I aim to serve."

I could not tell if Istina was upset, or curious, or both. I decided that my best option was to continue, so I plunged ahead. "Aletheia helps me search and fact-check information on the Internet. She's web savvy."

"It's an app?"

"Xeno-Scholar."

"I've heard of it. Software designed to ferret out Internet trolls?"

"That's her. Early prototypes exposed Russian trolls."

"How did you acquire it?"

"She was a gift." I smiled, remembering Mrs. Eyles. And then I wondered if Mrs. Eyles would approve of Istina. Of course. Would she approve of me having sex with Istina? Yes, if I used a condom to protect myself from disease, and Istina from pregnancy. And it was mutually consensual.

I couldn't suppress an ear-to-ear grin. I would send Mrs. Eyles an email tonight and start a discussion. I'd tell her about the age difference between Istina and me, and I'd ask her if it made a difference.

Ironically, my grin piqued Istina's curiosity.

"Well, let's test it out," Istina said. "What can it tell you about this mosaic?"

Aletheia said the Massacre of the Innocents was a story from the Gospels, based on a misreading of the Old Testament passage Jeremiah 31:15. Aletheia explained that the passage in Jeremiah was not a prophecy about children being killed, it was a passage about Rachel, the mother of two boys, weeping because her children were being taken to Egypt. Rachel's children were not being slaughtered. Subsequent verses in Jeremiah told how the children were returned, not murdered.

Christians reimagined the story for the New Testament and made up a story about the slaughter of children! What was in their minds as they reinterpreted the Old Testament story in such a shocking, violent way? Aletheia reported no historical evidence that such a slaughter actually occurred during the time of Christ, so the vile misinterpretation and subsequent lies were all the worse for it.

We wanted to ask Aletheia these questions, but we knew that she was unable to answer. They were not questions of fact. They were ethical and moral questions. Questions for humans to answer, not software programs.

We did ask Aletheia to find verses like "Thou shalt protect children from child abuse." She offered us the following: "I found no text in the Ten Commandments or the Old Testament about protecting children from child abuse or cruelty."

"I wouldn't be surprised if the Bible is pro-child killing," Istina stated, matter-of-factly.

"Hey Aletheia," I said, "provide verses documenting that the Bible is pro-child killing."

She responded instantly: "Hosea 9:14, Hosea 13:16, 2 Kings 15:16, Numbers 5:11-21, Numbers 31:15, Psalms 137:8-9, and 1Samuel 15:3." She then added an unrequested nexus, something that she had started doing during the past few days. "During the second Liberian civil war, 1999-2003, boy soldiers ripped open the wombs of pregnant women. In Hosea 13:16 God promises to destroy the infants of Samaria by ripping open the stomachs of pregnant women."

I gasped and Istina grimaced. We caught ourselves quickly surveying the church to see if anyone had over-heard Aletheia.

But Aletheia didn't stop. As if proud of herself, she added, "I also found nothing in the Bible about protecting people from slavery, genocide, and rape. Would you like a list of verses that are pro-slavery, pro-genocide, pro-rape?"

I waited for Istina's reaction. She remained quiet but shook her head.

"No!" I said. And then I asked Aletheia, "Are these terrible things promoted by the God of the Old Testament and Moses and his prophets?"

Aletheia answered, "Yes, promoted by God. Yes, promoted by Old Testament law. Yes, promoted by Moses. Yes, promoted by prophets. That is correct."

"Hey, Aletheia."

"Yes, Liko?"

I was silent for a few moments. During the silence Aletheia volunteered the following: "Liko, if you have concerns about unhealthy behavior in a relationship that you're in, or that someone you know is in, you may want to contact a Domestic Violence Helpline."

Istina and I locked eyes for a moment. We both forced a smile.

"Aletheia, thank you."

"Your satisfaction is all the thanks I need."

Istina said, "Morally, the Bible is outdated, especially the Old Testament. It's old hat."

"Well, what do you expect? It was written by and for a desert nomadic tribe. Not exactly a people that you'd find in today's world."

I added, "I never read the Quran. I read the Bible, though."

"I've read both."

"Most Christians haven't read the Bible," I said. "Do you know that the founder of the American Praise the Lord club did not read the entire Bible until he went to jail for accounting fraud? True, that's what he wrote in his autobiography."

Again, we looked around to see if anyone was listening, but no one seemed to be tracking our conversation. Or paying us any attention at all. If any of the people around us were Catholics, they were in their own world, ignoring us.

After we left the Duomo, we wandered through narrow, winding streets, back to the campo. Then we started back to the taxi stand.

On the way, tired and hungry, we stopped at Bar 4 Cantoni on Via di Citta. We ordered camomilla tea, café lattes, lasangna, risotto funghi porci, and a panforte margherita. I slipped the receipt into my pocket, a temporary souvenir for the day. I felt surprisingly happy to be with Istina.

While we were eating she asked me, "What do you

think of the Christian resurrection thing and everyone ascending into heaven? Do you believe that Jesus raised people from the dead?"

I replied, "Well, according to the New Testament, Jesus raised at least two people from the dead: Lazarus and the daughter of some other guy."

"Don't you wonder what happened to them? Did they show up at the crucifixion or something?"

"Like a couple of zombies?"

"Yeah. Did you know that the Gospel of Matthew talks about graves opening and the bodies of saints rising out of their graves? It happened right after Jesus' resurrection. The risen dead went into Jerusalem. Everybody saw them."

"Get out!"

"No. That's what the Bible says."

"And not a single historical mention of zombies walking around? Somebody would have written about it!"

We looked at each other, and then asked Aletheia.

"No," Aletheia concurred, "there is no historical document or record that graves opened and the bodies of saints arose, and that they came out of their coffins, and that they went into Jerusalem."

We both grew quiet.

I muttered, "Hercules dragged Alcestis back from death."

"What?"

"What do *you* think about the resurrection?" I asked her.

She smiled. "I believe in scientific resurrection of extinct species, but not individual people."

"What is scientific resurrection?"

"I have friends working on scientific resurrection. The mammoth genome. There is a Russian, Japanese, and

Korean team. They have mapped the genome of a mammoth found frozen in Siberia."

I didn't believe what I was hearing. Yet, I did.

"And the Neanderthal genome project. Some scientists at Harvard want to bring back—or at least learn more about—the Neanderthals."

"Were the Neanderthals religious?" I asked. "Do you know?"

"They buried their dead, at least some of the time."

"Would we be better off without religion?"

"Absolutely!" Istina replied. "Societal health? Check! Denmark, Norway, Sweden and even the Netherlands—all of which are largely atheistic—have better health care, better environmental protection. People live longer there. Atheists live longer! Infant mortality is lower, and so is crime. And there is better equality between people than even in your United States."

"I'm an atheist," I stated, matter-of-factly. For the first time in my life I was proud to be an atheist. As if to boast, I added George Bernard Shaw's oxymoronic, "And I thank God for it."

Istina grew silent.

"What happened in Rome?" I asked her. I held my breath, hoping to finally get an answer.

Istina took a long, deep breath, exhaled slowly, and then said, "My brother was attacked. And you saved us."

I recalled how well-matched they were, that I thought they made a good couple. "When I first saw your brother, I thought he was your boyfriend."

She smiled at that.

"Is he okay?"

"Yes, for now."

"Was it because of your research?"

My question surprised her, but she shook her head no.
"The protestors?"

"No."

"So, is your brother involved in something?

"No."

"Drugs? Gambling? Terrorism?"

"No."

I didn't understand. Why wouldn't she just explain? Why was she making it so difficult? So I asked point blank, my voice testy and edged with anger, "Istina, I killed a man in Rome . . . protecting you. I deserve an answer."

She folded her napkin and set it on the table. "I will tell you, but you must not get more involved. Do you understand?"

I wanted to reach across the table and shake her, but I stopped myself, barely. I had never shaken a person before. I said, "I understand. But I am already 'involved.'"

She frowned. "All right then." She took a deep breath and exhaled slowly. "My brother was not the first they attacked. Anyone who speaks out against the prophet Muhammad, the Quran, or questions the teachings of an Imam is targeted. Everyone knows of Salman Rushdie, the British Indian novelist? He wrote *The Satanic Verses* in 1988."

"I have heard of him. But I have not read *The Satanic Verses*."

"Did you know that Rushdie's translators and the publishers of *The Satanic Verses* were targeted?"

"No."

"A kindly, Japanese scholar was found stabbed to death in the hallway outside his office at a Japanese university. He had been stabbed over and over again on his arms, hands, neck, and face. It was a savage, barbaric, immoral attack on a gentle man who had a family."

"And Rushdie's Italian translator was stabbed in his apartment in Milan, Italy. He survived."

"And in Turkey, a crowd of Muslims set fire to a hotel in a failed attempt to kill a translator there, too. Many innocent people died in the hotel fire."

"And a publisher and a CEO of a publishing house in Norway were shot and injured. They survived."

"Incredibly, a man blew himself up, along with several floors of a hotel in Paddington, England, while making a book bomb."

We locked eyes. She wanted me to understand the gravity of what she was about to share with me.

"My brother is also a novelist and a hardline atheist, a lapsed Muslim. Back home he famously quoted Rushdie: 'My point of view is that of a secular human being. I do not believe in supernatural entities, whether Christian, Jewish, Muslim or Hindu.'"

I asked, "What is so terrible about not believing?"

She looked at me as if I was an idiot. "My brother is an apostate."

"What is an apostate?"

"Are you serious?" She turned away and faced the water. "Ask your Aletheia to Google it for you."

"Please, I want to understand. Why did they try to kill him? What did he do?"

"He stopped believing in Islam."

"I still don't understand. Many people stop believing in one religion or another. People change their beliefs all the time. I mean, as they learn about the world and have experiences. Why is that so bad?"

"Because the Imams have issued hadiths against apostates. One hadith says 'Whoever changes his religion, kill him.'"

"Well," I countered, "those Imams are idiots. They sound as morally bankrupt as America's white, evangelical Christians who profess Christian morality but voted for Trump."

She laughed. "Muslims tend to believe their hadiths, without questioning their Imams. Kind of like Catholics follow the guidance of their Pope. The hadith explains the sayings and actions of the Prophet."

She studied me before continuing. "Like you, Liko, I'm an atheist. I think it's all bunk, too. But there are many who believe."

I looked around. No one was listening.

"You know," I said, "Catholics and Christians excommunicate you. That can be cruel, socially, but they don't try to kill you. No physical violence. No assassination. Just shunning. Sometimes verbal abuse. Christianity is a little more civilized, don't you think?"

"Historically, no," Istina countered. "There were Inquisitions and witch trials. Non-believers were tortured and then publicly executed: hung, strangled, burnt alive. But it is true that most Muslims have not learned to stand up against other Muslims who issue immoral hadiths, politically inspired fatwas, or declare jihad. Millions of Muslims are silent."

She continued, "My brother was raised a Muslim, but he no longer believes. And I no longer believe. And many of our friends and colleagues no longer believe. My brother and I are *murtadd* – we publicly declared our unbelief."

"Are Muslims against your research, too? Against genetic engineering?"

"No. Ironically, no."

"Really? That surprises me."

"It surprises a lot of people. Islam is open-minded when it comes to science. My research offends neither Sharia principle nor law. Islamic scholars defer to medical experts and, in my case, to scientists."

"But I would think there would be some surra—some Islamic verses—that religious zealots would use against genetic engineering."

"No. Islam welcomes discoveries that 'alleviate the suffering of humanity.' It's surprising, but in this regard, Islam is less anal than Christianity."

I laughed out loud. Until that moment, I had not been aware of how tense our conversation had become.

I knew that Christians opposed research using embryonic stem cells because Christians believed that extracting cells from early stage embryos less than a week old was murder, even though the research might lead to a cure for Alzheimer's or Parkinson's. Christians meddle, slow down, and suppress research.

Istina continued, "Islam is okay with gene replacement. It's a little murky, though, when it comes to manipulating genes to change future generations, our future children and grandchildren, especially their physical appearance, intelligence, personality, and behavior. But Islam is not outright opposed. If it is in accordance with the Islamic legal maxim 'Qawaid Fiqhiyyah' it is permitted. All deeds are judged according to their intention."

"So how do you know if it is in permitted?"

"Well, that's an Islamic legal question, it's not a science question. I believe that genetic engineering is 'husn' – good, morally acceptable. It is not 'haram' – a prohibited act."

"Islam's tolerance surprises me," I said.

"Unless one starts playing around with pigs and pork." She laughed.

"But people *are* doing research with pigs, aren't they?" I asked. "For tissue and organ transplants?"

"When it comes to religion," she answered, "there is always a Catch-22."

My eyes scanned the faces of people we passed. I surveyed ahead of us, looking for any person that was suspicious, out of place, a possible threat. I puffed up as we walked, my chest out, my shoulders back. I placed my body between her and the street. Everyone in a business suit or too slovenly or too ordinary became a suspect. I listened to people talking, tried to identify their accents, but heard no Afrikaans.

"Have you ever done anything that upset Muslims?"

"I stopped believing."

"Nothing else?"

"No," she said, but she seemed unsure of her statement, as if remembering something. And then she remembered: "I did write a paper about Adam and Eve."

"Seriously?" I couldn't imagine that. I couldn't suppress my smile either. I almost laughed.

"Yes . . . I did." She sighed. "Actually it was more narrative and explanation. It was not research at all."

"Yeah?"

"I wrote it for Faisal. I wanted to impress my brother."

"Now I'm curious."

"Well, I used genetics to debunk the Christian claim that Adam and Eve were the first humans – the Primal Couple." She must have seen my incredulous look, because she quickly added, "It was based on fact and evidence and research that other scientists did. It wasn't original work. Just a summary of what other scientists had discovered. I wrote it in Arabic for Faisal."

"So?"

"Faisal published it on his blog."

"Really?"

"Yeah," she shook her head, clearly saddened by that.

"Can you explain it to me?"

"What?"

"Your summary."

"I'll try." She concentrated for a moment and then began. "Adam and Eve were not a Primal Couple. Geneticists have proven that mankind did not descend from just one man and one woman. Geneticists back-calculated. Starting with our known human genome and its diversity, geneticists back-calculated to a multitude of ancestors, many more than just two. And these ancestors lived at different times and places on the earth."

"How long ago?"

"It varies by chromosome and genes."

"How so?"

"For example, today men have a Y chromosome that goes back 100,000 to 300,000 years. Other genes and chromosomes have other dates."

"So genes are analogous to carbon dating?"

She smiled. "That's not really the best analogy."

I nodded.

"It means no primordial couple, no original sin."

My mind struggled to wrap around that. "So, you're saying that Adam and Eve did not actually exist as the first two people?"

"Correct. That conclusion is supported by evolutionary biology, too. If Jan was here he could explain it to you from an evolutionary perspective." Istina added, "In case you haven't figured it out yet, Christians hate evolutionary biologists more than any other scientists in the world."

I nodded. "I imagine that geneticists will soon be high on their list, too."

"Especially evolutionary geneticists." She laughed.

It wasn't funny, though I laughed too.

"At the end of the day," she said, "there is no compatibility between science and the Abrahamic religions."

"So," I continued. "No Adam and Eve, no original sin, no Fall, no need for salvation, no need for Jesus' crucifixion."

"You got it," she said, smiling. "There is mythical resurrection and there is scientific resurrection. Christianity is mythical. Genetics is scientific."

I understood. She absolutely wasn't safe.

Together, we hopped into the taxi. "Florence," I instructed. "Can you drive us to Florence?"

"Yes," the taxi driver agreed. He seemed pleased to receive such a large fare.

"Istina, we should go to my hotel?" I described it to her.

"Yes. That's a good idea," she agreed. "I would like that very much."

"Your hotel can transfer your luggage."

"Good idea." She phoned her hotel and made the arrangements.

Two 'good ideas' in a row: I felt like I was on a roll.

We soon arrived at my hotel in Florence. I frowned as I paid the taxi driver, knowing that the fare would not please my great-aunt. Yet, the trip had been worthwhile. I'd explain it someday to her.

After exiting the taxi, I led Istina into the lobby of the plush Al Palazzo Del Marchese Di Camugliano. I was in heaven that she was with me. But I was also worried about protecting her.

During the last minutes of the taxi ride, I had imagined us sharing one hotel room. I had imagined kissing her, clumsily but heartfelt. I also imagined giving her a foot massage with the foot cream. Then I imaged using the lotion from the hotel bathroom to caress her hands, kissing each finger as she offered them to me. Then I rubbed lotion onto her arms, her legs, her breasts, and the swale in the small of her back, her muscle-toned stomach . . . making love on the hotel bed. My body made her happy and that made me happy, too.

They had one room available and Istina was able to check in. Unfortunately it was Saturday and she could have the room for only one night: a guest with a weekly reservation was arriving tomorrow.

I was disappointed that she checked into her own room, that she did not share my room. How was I going to protect her if we were not together? But it made me consider the reality of our situation.

I wondered, too, should I try to kiss her, see if she was interested? She had held my arm as we strolled through Siena under the umbrella. On the other hand, I didn't want to make her angry again, like she was during the taxi ride to Siena. I decided to take things slow, see what happened.

I soon found myself sitting in a guest chair in her hotel room. She poured me a glass of white wine from the room bar. I took a sip—a sauvignon blanc. The small bottle stated "aromatics of citrus, gooseberries and passion fruit."

"Do you have ice?"

"For your wine?"

"Yes." I smiled. "I like my wine cold."

She laughed and handed me three ice cubes. I took them from her hand, brushing her fingertips. Wow! I slid the cubes carefully into my glass.

I didn't ask about her coworkers or Dr. Keyes, but the thought of them returning or showing up again, looking for us, interrupting us, all that troubled me. Besides, for all I knew, they were involved in the attacks. Did someone tip off the professional hit man who was waiting for Istina at the airport?

So I suggested: "Let's leave Florence."

"And go to Venice?" Istina countered, immediately.

"Great idea." Her suggestion delighted me. *Did she choose Venice because it was romantic?*

"My brother is somewhere safe. And I will be too, once I get to *The Veritas*. Until then we can hide in Venice."

I nodded again.

"In the meantime I want you to stay close to me, okay?"

"Sure. I can do that."

"But no more trouble. Okay? No more problems?"

Trouble? Problems? I didn't understand. Perhaps my face betrayed my confusion because she looked at me closer, as if taking the measure of me, judging me.

"You followed me to Florence, you crashed my conference and the dinner, you bullied Dr. Crisp and stole his glasses, you told Jan about the hit men and he ended up in the hospital. Don't do anything else without telling me first, okay?"

Her admonishment stung. *Was she scolding me?*

"Liko, I'm sorry, but you need to understand. My

research is expensive. *The Veritas* is extremely expensive. Don't frighten off my investors, okay?"

"I wouldn't do that." I looked at her. *Why was she treating me like a child? Was that what she thought of me? A child?* "I wouldn't do anything to hurt you or your research."

"Then don't."

Frustrated, I refilled my glass with wine and ice.

"I only attended the conference because I had to," she said. "I had investors I needed to meet. And it went well. And I had a presentation that I needed to give. And that went well, too." She paused and sipped her wine. "But now . . . now I need to get back to *The Veritas*."

Was it possible that her investors were Muslim? Was that the reason she was keeping quiet about the attack? Because the investors might become frightened and pull their funding for her research? It made sense. Was that why she didn't go to the police in Rome? Was that why she was trying to keep everything quiet?

"Who are your investors?"

"Liko, leave it alone." Her voice scolded me. "No more questions."

Her scolding hurt my pride yet again. I was doing my best. If I was bumbling along it was her fault, not mine. She wasn't sharing. She had given me no other choice.

Since she had a hotel reservation for only one night, we decided to leave for Venice the next day. Our plan—actually, her plan—was to hide out in Venice for a few days, then return to an airport. By then the men surely would have given up and left. And Istina could board a plane to Iceland and *The Veritas*. I would board a plane to my next European destination, perhaps Greece.

I now had mixed feelings about spending the next few days with her; she was a bit scary and overpowering. On the other hand, being around her was an adrenaline rush and I liked that. She kept me on edge. I liked that a lot.

As we finished the bottle of wine, I considered asking her if she wanted a foot massage, to relax, but it was now late and we were both tired. Besides, I didn't want another angry scene, so I went to my room.

Tomorrow morning we would leave for Venice! I anticipated awakening like a child on Christmas morning!

7

I woke early. The first thing I did, after shaving and show-ering, was check on Istina. I knocked. She opened the hotel door in silk pajamas.

"Are you hungry?" she asked. Of course I was. So she ordered room service for both of us. I ate my breakfast and half of hers. She pulled back the curtains and sunlight filled the suite.

After that she called Jan at the hospital and had a long talk with him. She got teary-eyed and worked several Kleenexes. As we had surmised, Jan had run into one of the men in the small two-story church near her hotel, Chiesa di Ognissanti, the Church of All Saints. The man was lighting a candle for an offering when Jan struck up a conversation. Of course the Afrikaner accent immediately gave the man away. The man must have been suspicious because he followed Jan out of the church and into the piazza. He stabbed Jan just before he could alert a police-man who was watching the protestors. She pushed the red end-call button on her phone, hanging up.

"Why would he stab Jan?" I asked.

"To protect his identity? He probably knows all about me and my brother, all about our family, friends, coworkers—everything. They will soon know all about you, too, if you're not careful."

"Who are they?"

"Professionals. Assassins."

"Muslims?"

"Maybe. Maybe not. Their motivation is money."

She added, "The doctors expect Jan to fully recover."

"That's great news."

"He asked about you. He asked me, 'How's the *young man* doing?'" She smiled.

Young man? I was past puberty.

"I told him you were fine."

But I wasn't fine. I was bored, except for her silk pajamas. She looked fantastic in them. They clung to every curve and crack of her body. And they were lavender, similar in color to her magenta leather coat.

"What's your favorite color?"

"Fuchsia," she answered. "What's *yours*?"

"Orange."

Fuchsia and orange: a loud and bold combination. I liked it. I glanced at the highlights in her hair until I found the orange ones again. I had never been around anyone like her, yet here I was in her suite, in Florence, and she was walking around in silk pajamas. And she was beautiful. I wanted to touch the silky fabric of her pajama top, brush the silk with my fingertips, place my hand casually on her shoulder and feel the silk against the palm of my hand. Would she let me, or would she pull away? That would be terrible, if she pulled away. I imagined that she would ignore me at first and then place her hand on top of mine. I'm an optimist.

We sat across the room from each other all morning. Istina read materials from the conference and I surfed the Internet and studied up on Venice. At noon we had lunch together, again room service.

I surmised that she wasn't letting me out of her sight for a minute, but I was okay with that. As long as she was with me, she was safe.

At 2:25pm we boarded the train from the S.M. Novella in Florence to S. Lucia, Venice. We travelled coach. I let her have the window seat: 18A. I saved our 38,00 Euro receipt. My suitcase was half-filled with receipts. The train ride and our arrival were uneventful; we saw no signs of the men in suits.

My first impressions of Venice: no cars, slower pace, more time. The only means of getting around was on foot or by slow motorboats and vaporetti.

On the train ride, I had asked Aletheia about the crime situation in Venice. She reported that Venice was one of the safest cities in Europe. Violent crime was very rare. And the police were not highly visible, like in Rome.

Aletheia reported that Venice was founded in the fifth century, built from land reclaimed from a swamp. She said Venice had once been a Roman area invaded by people from north of the Alps. The swamp and islands in the lagoon had provided some protection to the people here.

Today there were more than a hundred inhabited islands, almost two hundred canals, and a Grand Canal bent in the shape of an S, cutting through the city, dividing Venice into six districts, three on each side of the canal. And about 450 bridges! One could be anywhere in Venice in less than an hour.

Istina and I took separate rooms in a small hotel. Of course I found that disappointing, not only because of the additional cost, but also because on the train I had caught her staring at me. *We just need to work through some differences, that's all,* I thought.

But our differences were significant. She was accomplished. I was a high school graduate, barely. She was in her late thirties? I was almost nineteen. She was savvy, smart, and at the top of her game. I was eager. She was beautiful and I was . . . hopeful, optimistic. Did she think I was handsome? That would help.

After unpacking we got together again and dined at Lineadombra, which the concierge at our hotel front desk had recommended. We ate an appetizer of burrata cheese, a soft mozzarella, and arugula over artichoke heart with a dried tomato puree sauce. The cheese was topped with chopped truffles and drizzled with olive oil. It was served on a black plate, and with salt on the side. The restaurant was along the coast of Dordoduro overlooking Giudecca. We relaxed, drinking Peroni beers.

Istina wore slightly faded blue jeans with gold-tone metal pyramidal studs on top of each pocket, front and back. Brown stitching at her crotch. I couldn't keep my eyes off her. I was in awe! No other way to describe how I felt, the emotions, the incredible experience of being in her company. I felt privileged to be with her.

I asked her, "Can you talk about your research? What you and your team are doing? I saw top scientists from around the world at the conference."

"Let me answer by first asking you a question."

"Okay," I said.

"One theme of the conference was genetics and evolution. So let me ask you: What do you think we will become? Or more directly, what do you think our species will become?"

"You mean, if we control or direct the course of our own evolution?"

"Yes," she said.

I love biology and her question intrigued me. "I'd have to think about that. I don't want to give you a flippant answer."

I imagined that she had been pondering the question for some time: Now that we can control and direct our evolution, what will we become? I was pleased that she had asked my thoughts.

We were quiet for a moment, both enjoying the ocean view. And then I asked her, "What are *you* interested in? What is your research? In Siena you said something about scientific resurrection?"

"My research? To protect species at a genetic level, so scientists can one day resurrect them."

"Are you guys like mad scientists?

"Heavens no!"

"But someday scientists will grow a computer from human brain cells, right?" My question surprised her. "I saw that on one of the poster presentations at the conference. Another presenter proposed olfactory sensors grown from basset hound nose cells."

"It will not remain science fiction forever, Liko."

"I just don't understand it," I said.

"The nature of our genetic code is simple, amazingly simple. Each human being has only 46 chromosomes: 23 from our father and 23 from our mother. Now those 46 chromosomes contain about 23 thousand genes. All of it taken together is the human genome."

"I understand that DNA is the blueprint."

"Yes, DNA is the master plan for nature to build, maintain and repair human bodies. What is changed is our understanding of the genes. Scientists can now read the blueprint and manipulate our genes."

"Rewrite our human genome?"

"Yes," she said. "My colleagues and I have the tools and the technology to change the human genome and the genome of every other species that has lived, lives or will live upon the earth."

"So scientists can change everything about us: our appearance, intelligence, sexuality, behavior, even the choices we make, and our behavior."

"Scientists have already started."

Her statement reminded me of my conversation with Jan. He said scientists were already changing our human genome, too. That private money was funding their work. I recalled he was concerned about unintended mutations hurting babies. That was, indeed, a serious concern.

Istina excused herself to the bathroom. While she was away, I mentally compared myself with her accomplishments, her knowledge of genetics, her passion for her work and research. Was I trying to bolster my confidence? Or was I trying to find a weakness in her, one that would bring her down to my earthly level? I decided both.

I hadn't even gone to college yet! I had no work experience, except the Steakhouse. My accomplishments—learning how to swim, to scuba, to lift weights, and now to travel—were worthless compared to the resurrection of genomes and the modification of genes. What was my greatest accomplishment? Learning buoyance control in Hawaii?

I thought of my Uncle Keahi. Uncle was so indecisive. He worked at a State of Hawaii job that he disliked. He never pursued his dreams. He wasted his talents. Istina, on the other hand, had a deep sense of purpose, something that Uncle Keahi was struggling to rediscover.

I refused to be like my uncle! I wanted to do something important, significant, something like Istina and her team. Yes, that would make me happy. I wanted to be successful. For me, success meant reducing the suffering in the world.

Istina returned from the bathroom. I watched her walk to our table. She was absolutely wonderful. I was in awe of her—her body and yes, her mind and accomplishments. Sheer awe. Awe in the joy and beauty of her existence.

I gazed at her face as if paralyzed. Why was I feeling such turmoil? I thought about Hercules, my hero, and the son of Zeus. His appetite for women and wine and food. Great strength, adventures. A man who would do anything for a friend. But unlike Hercules, I wanted to be known and respected for common sense and good judgment. Of course, without Aletheia, I'd be as dumb as a bone relic.

8

Mid-morning sun brightened our mood, and I was proudly wearing my Prada sunglasses. Today Istina wore an embroidered pair of jeans. I had no doubt that they were handcrafted Italian. The jeans were tight and she looked fantastic.

We stood in the eastern end of the Piazza San Marco. The façade of yet another church stood in front of us. This one, I believed, was called Saint Mark's Basilica. Istina and I looked at it dead on.

I overheard a tour guide: "Here rest the remains of the evangelist Mark after a group of Venetian merchants went to Alexandria more than a thousand years ago and stole his body. They brought it back to Venice and built this church to honor him. Later the church burnt down."

Aletheia verified the facts, more or less. There was no evidence that the stolen body was the evangelist. The doges built him a church anyway. I'm not sure who the doges were, except that they were aristocrats. Aletheia equated doges to dukes. St. Mark's was essentially the church of the State of Venice, kind of like Westminster

Abbey is the church of the State of England. I had seen Westminster Abbey when I was in London. It was impressive. Similarly, it was here at St. Mark's that the aristocracy held their ceremonies: coronations, weddings, and lying in state after death. This was not the church of the common man.

Anyway, the church had burnt down several times, and St. Mark's relics had been lost in one of the fires, until rediscovered years later when his arm appeared with a ring on it, miraculously sticking out of a pier. Give me a break!

As we entered through the central portal, I saw a mosaic of Noah. That didn't surprise me. After all, Venice was prone to flooding.

It was noon, yet not a lot of natural light entered the church. Many windows appeared closed up. Perhaps that was why it was artificially illuminated with electric lights.

I saw the shiny Pala d' Oro altarpiece, shiny gold and precious stones, biblical characters dressed in blue robes. Even Jesus was dressed in blue. Golden halos surrounded their heads like space helmets. Jesus had both a halo of gold and a halo of gems. I saw a row of effeminate angels, turned sideways to me, with large wings from the top of their head to their knees. Each character—saints, Jesus, angels, Mary, evangelists, apostles and probably even a doge or two—were set in individual arched niches, most standing full frontal against a gold background, all framed by sparkling gemstones, more than a thousand emeralds, garnets, and sapphires. And a thousand pearls.

Next we went downstairs to see a crypt. Someone said that the relics were brought out and shown off at Easter. Human bones no longer impressed me. In my short lifetime there would be billions more.

Just before one o'clock, we paid eighteen Euro to see the

Museo Di Piazza San Marco and, once again, I slipped a receipt into my pocket.

Four life-sized horses stunned me. Equestrian muscle cast in copper. Veins visible, powerful.

Aletheia said the horses were gelded and I verified that: they were indeed castrated. Never considered that was done to horses. Makes them less aggressive, like dogs and cats, I guess. Still, they were magnificent.

Sadly they were plundered from the Fourth Crusade of 1202 to 1204. Aletheia provided us a quote. I put her on speaker so we could both listen to her quote Steven Runciman: "There was never a greater crime against humanity than the Fourth Crusade."

As unexpected as a bolt of lightning flashing through a blue sky, Aletheia volunteered the following: "Liko, I found something that might interest you. The Crusaders destroyed a bronze statue of Hercules. Lysippos created the statue."

"Aletheia, who was Lysippos?"

"Lysippos was court sculptor to Alexander the Great in the fourth century BC."

"Why did they destroy the statue?"

"Crusaders melted the large statue to make coins."

"Do you have a picture of the statue?" I realized that was a silly question as soon as I asked it. I hoped Istina wouldn't think me stupid.

"A picture of the destroyed Hercules is not available on the Internet. However this is a photograph of the Farnese Hercules." I heard a ping as the picture appeared on the phone. "The Farnase Hercules is a copy of Lysippos' colossal marble statue of Hercules, resting on his club after his labors." And then Aletheia added an additional morsel.

"The Horses of Saint Mark may be copies of Lysippos' work, too."

I gazed at the magnificent marble sculpture of Hercules on my phone, and then the copper stallions on display in front of me, and I realized that a bronze masterpiece of Hercules had been destroyed during the Fourth Crusade. I shared the picture of the Farnese Hercules with Istina and then saved it to my photos. It would always be a reminder to me of the stupidity of Christian religious intolerance and human greed.

We both found the dungeons beneath the Gothic Doge's Palace disturbing. The torture chamber filled me with anger. I told Istina, "It reminds me of Gitmo and waterboarding." Istina was interested in the fact that Casanova, while only 30 years of age, had been imprisoned in a cell on the top floor in 1755 for being 'disrespectful of religion and common decency.' She was impressed that he had escaped to Paris.

After we exited the Gothic palace, we found ourselves standing before the execution posts in the Piazzetta di San Marco: two large granite columns topped by statues of St. Theodore and St. Mark. Now it was Istina's turn to be upset. I don't know why she found them so disturbing, though. I wanted to ask her, but I balked.

Instead, I invited her to join me for tea, and she accepted. We strolled across the piazza, disturbing a few pigeons. The waiter seated us at a front row table facing the piazza and took our order of tea and croissants. "You chose a famous restaurant," she said, pleased.

When the tea arrived she volunteered her thoughts: "The statues of St. Theodore and St. Mark are so pagan, their falseness infuriates me. Why don't people see the nexus between these semi-Christian statutes and their pagan origins? Doesn't science now separate us from this nonsense?"

I liked the sparks in her hazel eyes and the anger in her voice, as long as it wasn't directed at me. I wanted to ask her more about herself, more about her beliefs, more about everything. I wondered, if I shared something personal about myself would she reciprocate? Perhaps if I shared something intimate. Perhaps that would help her open up, share with me? I thought it worth a try.

So I began a stream of conscious monologue. "I don't have any brothers and sisters. I grew up in a trailer park just outside Las Vegas. Almost half the seniors in my high school class failed to graduate. I was lucky. The kids who didn't graduate couldn't read. I think most of them got low-wage jobs on the strip. They hustled tourists. That's what I escaped from."

Istina said, "I see."

I continued. "My Uncle Keahi lives in Hawaii. He ignored me until I was a sophomore. Since then, he has tried to make it up to me for not helping me earlier. He should have taken custody of me when I was in grade school. He had to have known that my parents were alcoholics and my dad was abusive. Instead, I was the one who had to plan my escape from my mother and her trailer park.

"My great-aunt, she is amazing. You would like her. You know you are blessed when you meet someone who knows you better than you know yourself. Well, that's my great-aunt. She is a kind and generous person. She is paying for this world trip of mine.

"I have an agreement with her, it's a no-strings-attached deal. She pays for my travel for one or two years, and then I return to Hawaii, maybe go to university. She's already offered to pay my tuition wherever I decide to go. I've been thinking about biology, specifically marine biology, maybe even oceanography. I guess, for me, the ocean is my passion. Just like genetic engineering is for you."

Istina nodded.

"I didn't have a happy childhood. My mother wasn't there for me. My father was a run-of-the-mill domestic abuser. Nothing special about him, whatsoever. I feel sorry for my mother, though. I can't remember a time when she was happy. Maybe when she was younger. Maybe she was in love with my father then. But she lost respect for him. She knows that he doesn't respect her. When I was old enough to understand, I realized that he was embarrassed by her, by her homely appearance and lack of social graces. She is not attractive, I admit that. She is big-boned. Broad nose. Wild hair." I smiled and paused for effect. "Like me."

Istina brushed her long braids off her shoulder and smiled. She tilted her head slightly. Even her simple moves were graceful.

"Istina, if you could change anything about the way you were raised, what would it be?" I paused for a moment but not long enough for her to answer. Instead I continued, "For me, I wish I had grown up in my great-aunt's home. I wish that I had run away when I was younger, like Keahi, and been taken in by my great-aunt, too. I wish that I had not waited until my sophomore year.

"If my mother's apartment caught fire—she now lives in an apartment because I moved her from her trailer into an apartment just before I started this trip—I'd save her. But I would not rush back in to save any of our stuff. That's how poor we were. We didn't even have memories worth saving! No pictures. No home movies. No vacation trinkets. I have nothing material to lose. Kind of freeing, in a way."

Istina gazed at me. I caught multiple emotions on her face: affection, curiosity, concern.

"I was the fat kid, not athletic. Picked on by everyone for being obese and clumsy." I forced a smile and again paused for effect. "But I've grown out of that."

"I feel bad about my Uncle Keahi, because I never thanked him for the summer vacations and for saving my life twice. I owe him big time. I hope to find a way to pay him back. I failed to treat him well. I disappointed him. Besides, my uncle never learned to live. I care about him."

I grew quiet and waited for Istina to respond, to say something. She surprised me by remaining silent. I had just shared intimate details of my life. I had saved her life in Rome. What more could I do to win acceptance?

We spent the remainder of the afternoon in yet another museum. Actually we toured an administrative palace of some kind, which I found immensely boring. We walked from one grand room to another grand room until the overwhelming richness of paintings, furnishings, and architecture all became . . . grandly boring.

Sunset found us at Caffe La Piscine, seated at a waterside table. A stunning view. We sipped sparkling water. And then I really opened up emotionally. I told her, from my heart, all about the girl who had drowned in the flooded quarry. It had been my responsibility to warn her about the hazards. I hadn't. My eyes watered, but I kept my composure.

"Let's go for a gondola ride!" she suggested, perhaps to cheer me up—or to shut me up.

"That's a great idea!" I blew my nose into the napkin. I knew it wasn't a very cultured thing to do, but it was necessary. I did it quickly, folded the napkin and placed it next to my plate. I paid the bill, pocketed the receipt for the lasagna, mazzancolle, and maialino, and off we went to find a gondola.

Riding in the gondola, I felt ecstatic. I was also alert, as if my body was pumped up on amphetamines. I thrust out my chest. I was a human shield. I would protect her!

It was nighttime, the optimal time for gondola riding, and Istina was seated beside me. I finally found the courage to place my arm around her shoulders. She let me. She even held my free hand comfortably in her lap.

We glided through a city in decay, passing damp and rundown buildings, picturesque canals, gloomy alleys. I sensed decay all around me. Seated in the gondola, we saw the shifting reflections of Venice on the surface of tired canals.

I didn't want to think about global warming. Or the Experimental Electromechanical Module, which the concierge at our hotel called the MOSE project, and which may or may not save Venice from sea level rise. The MOSE project consisted of rows of mobile gates that someday would open and close with the rising and lowering of the tides—gates that would keep the high tides in the Adriatic Sea and out of the Venetian Lagoon, just as Moses separated the waters in the Red Sea. But would it work if the sea rises ten feet? Fifteen feet? We didn't want to think about it.

9

The next day, we strolled side-by-side until we found ourselves standing in front of yet another church. This one was Gothic: Basilica St. Maria Gloriosa dei Frari, or simply the Frari.

"Inside is Titian's tomb," Istina told me. "And the Assumption of the Virgin, Titian's painting of Mary rising into heaven. It is beautiful and fantastical."

She wanted to see the inside of another church. Who was I to argue? However, I declared, "I hope this is the last church."

"Okay," she agreed. "We'll make this our last."

Aletheia told us the Frari was built in 1330. She said that Titian was buried inside. He had died of fever during an outbreak of plague in Venice in the 1500s. She also told us that his 22-foot oil painting of Mary passing into eternal life was considered a Renaissance masterpiece. The painting had established Titian as "the master of light and shadow and shifting colors, colors that are rich and deep." So I braced myself for what I was about to see.

I liked the simplicity of the church and its bell tower. I

remarked about the pointed arch above the doorway and the Madonna above the arch. As we entered, I looked down the long nave, past the wooden choir seating, and to the altar where I discerned a semi-dome and side chapels. And an enormous painting: the Titian.

I walked towards it. The figures were larger than life size: three dimensional and visible from the front and behind. A woman wore a bright red robe. The palms of her hands rose skyward. A blue mantle girdled her red robe and was tied in a knot in front of her twisted body. She was standing on a half-wreath made of clouds, held mid-air by fat cherubim with green wings that resemble evergreen leaves. She stood in front of an aurora of golden light.

Not bad, I thought as I walked down the knave towards the giant painting.

The woman gazed upwards into the eyes of a man who floated above her. On the man's right a small fat cherub held a dark crown.

I got it—the man with the windblown hair was the father of Jesus, and the woman gazing into his eyes was Mary, who he had impregnated some 30-plus years before. He was the Christian God. He was about to crown her and she appeared surprised. He appeared stoic and lacked any expression of love, joy, or peace. I imagine she was surprised because he was not her husband Joseph. I asked myself: Whatever happened to Joseph and all the rest of Mary's sons and daughters? According to myth, this god had snatched her into the troposphere either before she died or before her dead body decayed—one or the other.

I found the whole thing insulting, including the men below Mary who were excited, frantic, and dramatically gesturing.

I turned to Istina, "I like the marble frame."

"You're hopeless," she joked. She took my arm and we walked slowly back towards the church entrance. I was ecstatic that she had taken my arm.

"The assumption of Mary into heaven has been debated for centuries," Istina said. "The Pope made it *de facto* Catholic dogma in the Fifties."

On the way out we glanced at Donatello's wooden carving of St. John the Baptist, but we hardly stopped. It was clear that we were burned out on Christian architecture, paintings, and sculpture.

We ate lunch at a sandwich shop overlooking a small footbridge and the basilica, and then we shared a small cup of gelato. As we walked back to our hotel, we stopped to listen to two fabulous guitar players outside the Scuolo Grande San Rocco and buy their CD. In the Scuolo we rented an audio guide and learned about the fraternity system of upper middle class Venetians who gained stature by pooling their resources.

We decided not to visit the adjacent church. We both agreed that we had seen enough churches for a lifetime, and enough Christian art for several lifetimes.

Late afternoon found us on a tour of the Teatro La Fenice, the Venetian opera house. "It's splendid," Istina exclaimed as we stood in the Royal Box gazing out into the House. The red and gold and Rococo style house contrasted with the dark green velvet-like stage curtain directly in front of us. Gilt leather flowers floated down the curtain like autumn leaves. A gilt bronze chandelier hung from the ceiling. Gold leaf acanthus leaves choked the house and boxes like wild ivy growing everywhere, even on the ceiling, as if searching for sunlight and heaven. Nine beautiful women and three cherubs floated on the ceiling, circling the chandelier, playing string instruments, filling Istina and me with joy. Next, the tour guide ushered us through one spectacular room after another: the five rooms of the Sala Apollinee dedicated to Apollo, including the Sala Grande where our tour interrupted a public meeting being held in the ballroom, and the Sala Dante with its main bar; the Sala Rossi with a reproduction of the Basilica Palladiana along the walls as if one were standing in the central Piazza dei Signori in Vicenza; and the newer exhibition and rehearsal rooms. All impressive. All overwhelming. Istina loved it, and that made me happy.

Unfortunately, at the end of the tour, when Istina tried to buy opera tickets for the evening performance of La Bohème, they were sold out. She was extremely disappointed.

I tried to cheer her up with a dinner nearby, but the pizza was thin and cold. Afterwards we shopped, exploring small artisan shops. I thought she would like that, but she didn't buy anything. I wanted to buy her a souvenir to remember our time together in Venice, but I didn't find anything. Ironically, after an hour of shopping, we found ourselves again in Campo San Fantin, facing the neo-classical colonnade of the Teatro La Fenice.

It had grown dark. We were tired from being on our feet all day, and now we had a long walk back to the hotel ahead of us.

We gazed up at the theater's insignia, a phoenix rising from the flames. During our earlier tour we had learned that the theater had burned and been rebuilt several times. An arson in 1996 had destroyed the stage, ceiling, and many of the tiers of box offices. Two statues stood in niches on each side of the phoenix: the muse of tragedy and the muse of dance. The masks of Comedy and Tragedy also looked down upon us, laughing and crying.

"Istina, I have a present for you." I handed her a white envelope. She opened it and took out both a card and a smaller brown envelope.

She read the card. "That's sweet," she said. The card proclaimed my friendship for her. She closed the card and gave me a kiss on the cheek. She then tore open the brown envelope. She took out two items, tickets. She read them and exclaimed "La Bohème? Tonight?"

Yes, with the help of our hotel concierge I had scored tickets to La Bohème on the day that we arrived in Venice. I had racked my brain to find something special for Istina. I was now happy!

And then she surprised me. She threw both her arms around my neck and pulled herself up and me down and planted a kiss on my forehead. I floated for a moment, suspended between earth and sky.

Istina loved the performance. I discovered that she loves opera. They say that true opera lovers cry during performances. She cried.

10

The following day, I stood in front of van Gogh's *Mountains of Saint-Remy* in the Peggy Guggenheim Museum, which was a remodeled 18th century Grand Canal palazzo. This was the first van Gogh that I had seen in real life and I was absolutely blown away! I gazed at the same mountains that van Gogh had seen from his mental hospital. He painted them, and the next year he killed himself.

"Superb," I said.

"Did you know that van Gogh's great-grandnephew, Theo van Gogh, was murdered in Amsterdam?"

"No," I answered.

"A man shot him eight times while he was bicycling to work in the morning. And then attacked him with a knife. Tried to cut his head off."

"Why?" I asked. "Why would someone do something so terrible?"

"Because Theo made a movie that criticized Islam, focusing on the treatment of women in Islamic society. The name of the short movie is *Submission*. It is about Muslim women suffering abuse."

"Have you seen it?"

"Yes, it's on YouTube."

We enjoyed the oil painting a while longer and then she added: "Theo dressed an actress in a semi-transparent burqa and then he painted verses on her body in henna, on her naked skin. Verses from the Quran that Muslims use to justify the subjugation of women. And violence against women. The film pissed off a lot Muslims."

With that she paused. I overheard a docent comment about Vincent van Gogh's painting. She said something about acrylic paints being a breakthrough because they allowed artists to paint more easily in the countryside. I imagined Vincent van Gogh took full advantage of that. The docent said something about acrylic freeing the artists from the slower drying oils, which made canvases harder to manage.

"Did they threaten him?"

"Yes, but Theo did not take the threats seriously."

"How about you? Did someone threaten you? Your brother?"

"Yes. And now you are involved, too."

I gazed at the painting, and then asked Aletheia to find a quote by a famous biologist that I admire, Edward O. Wilson. I thought it would be relevant. Besides, I hoped to impress Istina. "Would they be interested in finding the truth that Nietzsche called, in *Human, All Too Human*, the rainbow colors around the outer edges of knowledge and imagination?"

"What does that mean?" Istina asked.

"We must all seek the truth, just as Vincent van Gogh, his great-grandnephew Theo, and so many great artists in this gallery have done. I hope that Muslims will seek the truth, too."

Istina looked at me kind of strangely. I wondered if I had said something really stupid again.

She said, "You are more optimistic than me." She broke into a smile.

I felt giddy and full of life, like being narked. I said, "Someday, most of the characters in our sacred books—Jewish, Christian, and Muslim—will be myths, just like the Greek and Roman gods and their stories and literature are myths."

She added, "The sooner they become myths, the better."

We both smiled.

I reached over and took her hand. She let me! Such a simple thing, holding another human being's hand, yet so amazing, so comforting. And so electrifying.

Istina now introduced me to the most popular collection of contemporary art in Venice. As we walked through the Peggy Guggenheim Collection, my mind transitioned from glittery gold mosaics, atmospheric church lighting, and religious paintings, which I had overdosed on during the previous week, to a collection of contemporary art.

Istina lead me to a freestanding terra cotta bust of a woman. I read the nameplate: *Head of a Young Woman*, by Henri Laurens.

We were still holding hands. We slowly walked around the sculpture. Suddenly the principles of cubism snapped into place. Seeing cubism in 3-D made all the difference! I squeezed her hand. It dawned on me that she was my art guide today. I was happy to follow and learn.

When we came to Jackson Pollock's *The Moon Woman*, I wanted to share my new insight. "I can see her face from two points of view: from the side and straight on. I get it now. Before today, I'd look at one of these pictures and it made no sense, whatsoever. But now I get it."

I continued, explaining what I thought I had learned: "From one angle the woman has it together: she seems content, composed. Like you. But maybe that is just the side that you present when you are in public, that you let everyone see. From the other angle, the woman is sad, thoughtful. That could be you when you are alone and thinking and no one is around to disturb you. Maybe you are thinking about your research. Maybe you are wondering if your experiments are ethical."

She squeezed my hand.

"Maybe I'll call you my Moon Woman."

"What do you think of this one?" she said, pointing at the next painting with her free hand. It was a wild and crazy painting. I read the nameplate: Jackson Pollock.

"I can't believe the same guy did this one," I said. I looked it over. The oil on canvas was named *Enchanted Forest*. But there was no forest. "It looks like Aletheia's neural network, if she had one."

Istina laughed out loud. "I like that."

Later we came to Max Ernst's oil on canvas, *The Antipope*. "Horse people? Is this a possibility now? Part horse, part human? Will your research make that possible?"

"Eventually, yes. But I doubt anyone would want the head of a horse. Not even horse lovers." She stated that too matter-of-factly for my comfort.

"Well, what about this one? " I pointed out *The Break of Day* by Paul Delvauz, an oil painting. It showed naked women. Their upper bodies were human and their full, round breasts were spectacular. Their lower bodies were trees, though. They appeared rooted in place. "You know

there is a Greek myth about a nymph that turns into a lau-
rel tree. Could you guys make something like that? A creature part human and part plant?"

I waited for her reply, but I didn't take my eyes off the
painting. I made another comment: "Their eyes look dull,
unfocused. Perhaps they are suffering from a new medical
condition, cellulose on the brain?"

"Redwoods live tens of thousands of years." She smiled.
"Perhaps there will be some kind of trade-off."

"You've got to be kidding!"

"No, I'm not kidding. Some people will do anything to
live longer."

"And how about this one?" she said. I recognize it as
another Jackson Pollock. We held hands and stood
motionless in front of it. "It's exceptional!"

"Pollock squeezed paint out tubes onto the canvas,"
Istina said. "Or maybe he poured paint."

"Or both," I said. "I like it. I like it a lot."

Together we stood looking at it for a full five minutes,
as if hypnotized. Our eyes followed rhythmically the broad
thick paint strokes. We felt the texture of the paint.

And then I saw the eyes staring back at us. The eyes of
animals! Surprised, I stretched so I could read the nameplate while holding Istina's hand firmly in mine. The
nameplate said *Eyes in the Heat.*

"Do you see them?"

"What?"

"The eyes."

"Get out!"

"Oh yeah. Their eyes are watching us. The eyes of the
extinct species that scientists will resurrect. The eyes of
endangered and threatened species that are destined for

your gene banks. The eyes of our children and their children. All of their eyes are on YOU, Istina."

"Liko!" She grabbed my upper arm, my bicep, in both her hands and shook me. "Don't make fun of me! Or my work! Besides, I don't scare that easily."

I put my arm around her and pulled her against me, pressing the side of her body against mine. I was in heaven.

We proceeded to the museum restaurant. When we were seated Istina said, "Yesterday you told me about your parents and what it was like growing up in a trailer park outside of Las Vegas."

"Yes," I tried to say the one word 'yes' with as much encouragement as I possibly could.

"Well, today it is my turn."

Hurrah! My patience had paid off. Istina, please, please, open up!

"Your parents were not very loving. Perhaps your mother was? I don't know. But I had very loving parents. My brother and I were raised in an affluent Muslim home, went to mosque weekly, and did the community prayer with our Saudi neighbors.

"Unlike your parents, my parents were very religious people. My father spent a lot of time praying and reciting the Quran. My mother was quiet, obedient, and pious.

"My older brother, Faisal, he questioned everything. He is brilliant and intellectually fearless. He debated with everyone and questioned everything. He is a genuine critical mind, seeking knowledge and truth. After my father, Faisal is my hero.

"My brother studied the Quran and the hadiths. I have happy memories of him sharing verses with me that pointed to peace and love and justice. I have sad memories of other times, though, when he would weep, sharing verses with me that pointed to intolerance, hatred, and violence. We wept. And we learned.

"My brother came to the conclusion that Islam is a violent religion. Even though the majority of Muslims are peaceful, it is the politically and religiously radicalized Muslims who dominate.

"My brother and I read the Quran and discussed the Sira together. We saw how peaceful verses were preceded and superseded by violent verses. Context is important! And the violent verses are more numerous.

"We both came to the conclusion that Sharia law is not good, especially for women. I learned this from personal experience growing up in Saudi Arabia, traveling throughout the Arab world, and going to universities in democratic and even former communist countries where people have freedom of religion."

"Like your brother," I said, "I too believe in rational inquiry. Perhaps there will an Islamic reformation."

"Sadly," Istina said, "it takes just one suicide bomber in a gathering of peaceful Muslims to destroy many worlds. One suicide bomber who feels under siege, victimized, and exploited. One suicide bomber who does not reflect rationally on the Quran. One suicide bomber who is unable to question anything that a desert warrior said 1,500 years ago, but can only follow Muhammad's example. One suicide bomber hypnotized by fatwas, calls to jihad, unenlightened hadiths, and defunct holy books. One suicide bomber who believes Islam is under siege and blames others. A simple-minded person who does what the texts say because he or she does not exercise his own judgment as a moral being."

"Perhaps," I said, "given time Islam will evolve.

She took my forearm in both of her hands. She held my arm securely. "Liko, you are such an optimist! A thousand years ago some Muslim philosophers tried to reform Islam. They were wiped out. Today the enemy of peaceful Islam comes to worship wearing a suicide vest."

She recited several verses from memory:

"Profit, make war on the unbelievers and hypocrites and deal rigorously with them. Hell shall be their home: and evil fate." Quran 9:73

"Believers, make war on the infidels who dwell around you. Deal firmly with them. Know that god is with the righteous." Quran 9:123

"It is sad but not hopeless," I said. "Someday there will be a reformation. Eventually all the Abrahamic religions will be just myths."

"In the meantime, there are horrifically violent criminals out there," she said.

"There will always be people who pursue the truth and ask for evidence. I am one of them. You are one of them. Your brother is one of them too. People are joining us. Many Christians and Jews no longer believe the tenets of their religions. If they can undergo such a transformation, surely the Muslims can, too."

"I hope so, Liko."

After we left the museum restaurant, we passed through one more exhibit area where we discovered three works by Alberto Giacometti: *Woman Walking, Piazza,* and *Woman with Her Throat Cut.* All in bronze. All shocking.

Istina once again squeezed my hand, tightly.

The *Piazza* was a miniature-scale bronze of four men walking through a piazza. A single woman stood among them, unmoving, back straight. All of the figures were thin and tall.

We looked at each other and when our eyes met, we knew that we were having the same thought. This was Istina and the three men who attacked her.

I wondered, was the fourth man her brother, or was it me? Or was it someone else?

Istina gasped. She had seen the next sculpture. I followed her eyes and then I saw it. It was not quite life size, maybe 3 feet long and a foot high. A woman lay on her back. Her throat cut, her legs were spread wide open, and her pelvis arched upwards in grotesque agony. Her mouth was open. Was she crying out in pain? For help?

Still holding hands, I led her around the bronze sculpture. Now it looked like an insect. Perhaps a praying mantis? A praying mantis sprayed with chemicals, in its death throes?

We walked a little further. Now it looked like the backbone and body had separated from the exoskeleton, which was left behind on the ground. Like lobster meat pulled from the tail shell. Or a smashed cockroach? What the hell was it?

"I'm here. I'll protect you."

"I know you will, Liko. But the safest place for me is aboard *The Veritas*, my research vessel." She looked at me. Squeezed my hand even tighter. "You know, I need to get back to my work. A lot of people depend on me." She released my hand.

I wanted to argue, but I knew that it would make no difference. She was passionate about her work, and she would hate me if I kept her from it. I just nodded my head. "I'll look after you until you leave, okay?"

"Sure," she said, smiling.

We left the Peggy Guggenheim Museum. We were tired, so we headed directly back to the hotel.

But when we passed a Venetian mask store, Istina pulled me in. Wonderful costumes and accessories. India ink, gold leaf, plumes, macramé. Papier-mâché masks.

Istina purchased a pig mask for herself and an owl mask for me.

I looked around me. I was surrounded by all kinds of earthly and mystical creatures. Why hadn't I noticed this before? "Cool," I said. "I think I'll like masquerades."

When we returned to our hotel she invited me into her room. The first thing she did was go to the bathroom. I could hear her pee. This was a first for me, hearing a woman make water.

When she came out she was crying. For some reason, unknown to me, I started crying too. Perhaps because we knew we were soon to part—her to Iceland and the *RV Veritas*, me to the next adventure on my European tour.

Still crying, she sat down. I sat down next to her. I wrapped my arms around her and hugged her. She nestled her head into my chest, her hair exploding everywhere. I loved it! She inhaled, smelled my body odor, and said, "You smell wonderful." I buried my nose in her thick braids and said, "You too!" We sat and held each other for a long time, content, and wonderfully happy.

We had no wine. Nothing alcoholic.

She wanted me, and I wanted her, badly. We removed our clothes and soon stood facing each other naked. We hugged. I bowed my head to her, closed my eyes, and inhaled deeply. The salts from her body smelled like the ocean, alive, turbulent, overpowering.

We kissed, and I carried her into the bedroom and to the four poster bed. The cover was already turned down, and I laid her on top of the soft sheets.

We slowly and gently made love.

Afterwards as she rested her head on my chest, her cheek resting on my left pectoral muscle, as if I was her pillow, her knees on either side of my hips, her thighs spread apart wide, while I was deep inside her, I was happy. I believe that she was happy, too.

Lying on top of me, Istina said, "Our bodies know each other."

I agreed. I wrapped my arms around her, hugging her, cradling her the best that I could, holding her body against mine—no, encouraging her to rest her body on top of mine.

I nestled her into the contour of my left arm, steadying her on top of me, while my right hand caressed the back of her thighs, the sexually charged curve of her buttocks, the small, concave swale at the base of her back.

And then I wrapped her up in my arms in a primordial hug. My desire was to hold her in my arms in safety. To hold her in a way that gave her absolute comfort and peace—a primordial peace. I thought to myself, *you are safe in my arms.*

And then she rolled off of me onto the bed sheets.

Her body was fantastic. Fit, trim, strong.

My body on the other hand . . . "I'm nervous about my body."

"Liko, you have a fantastic body. You have a great body."

"No one has ever told me that before."

"I know genes, Liko. You have great genes!"

"Istina, you're beautiful."

"Thank you."

As we lay in bed together, we talked about our plans, and the topic of her safety came up. Again she told me, "The best place for me is aboard *The Veritas*. It is also the safest." It was like a broken record, now.

"I've heard of your ship but I don't know anything about it."

"It's a research vessel set up for genetic engineering experiments. It is designed to stay in international waters, indefinitely."

"Is it a hazardous ship?"

"Hazardous?"

"You know, hazardous chemicals, infectious organisms. Does it have stuff like that on board?"

"No, none of that. There is no risk of pathogens escaping from our labs, or any of us becoming infected." She paused. "We don't work with pathogens. We have no disease organisms on board."

"Why do you keep the ship in international waters?"

"To keep governments from interfering with our research. Including the United States. And because of protesters. I mean, you saw the protesters in Florence."

"Where is *The Veritas*?" I knew it was somewhere near Iceland.

"Ah . . ." she smiled, "if I tell you . . ."

"You'll have to kill me?"

"Something like that." She smiled and we both laughed at the lame reference to an old joke.

"What is *The Veritas* like?"

"She has an icebreaker hull, so she can go into the polar regions. In fact, she was originally designed for polar research. In particular, oceanographic research."

I found that interesting. "Maybe I could get a job aboard?"

"I'd like that. Someday I'll show you the ship. But first you must get your degree. Learn the basics of organismal biology, biochemistry, and genetics. I can't tell you where she is, but right now she is being extensively retrofitted. My next research requires specific modifications. She has been redesigned from bow to stern by colleagues at Beijing University and with assistance from friends at the University of California Davis."

"You know I love the ocean, but I don't know about labs or working aboard a ship."

"Liko, one of the earliest research vessels was the *HMS Resolution*. Her captain was Captain Cook." She smiled. "Heard of him?"

"Every Hawaiian knows about Captain Cook," I said. "But I didn't know he was doing research."

"They were studying planetary movements, not genetics, but they also had botanists on board. Two botanists who collected plants from all over the Pacific."

"Someday . . ."

"Liko, you are very special."

I smiled. "I love you, Istina."

I allowed my right hand to rest on her hip, and then she fell asleep.

11

I awake in bed. Sunlight is already coming in through the gap in the heavy window curtains. I roll from my left side to my back and stretch out my arm, expecting to find Istina lying beside me. She is not there.

Was it a dream? No! I am still here in the hotel bed. But she is no longer beside me.

I lay quietly in bed, expecting to hear noises from the bathroom. The sound of her peeing and washing her hands. But all is quiet.

Did she leave me? But then I tell myself that that is ridiculous. Everything was fine when we fell asleep.

I get up on my side of the bed and modestly pull on my boxer underwear, the pair with the pattern of smiling whales on them. I stroll into the bathroom. She is not there. Her toothbrush and a green package of dental floss rest on a neatly folded washcloth, next to the sink bowl.

I return to the bedroom and open the window curtains and morning sunlight floods the room. The light reveals her suitcase. It is still on the divan where the hotel porter placed it when we first arrived, so it would be easy for her to get her stuff.

I look in the clothes closet. Her embroidered pants and an orange blouse are missing. I have to smile at myself, acknowledging that I know her clothes. Her pants, shirts, socks, shoe size. Being interested and curious about her, I have made a mental note of all her possessions. I especially like the embroidered pants, with the hand-embroidered flowers.

I wonder where she went so early in the morning? Maybe she woke up hungry after our night together. Yeah, I bet that's it. She woke up famished. But where would she go this early in the morning? Perhaps the local bakery for warm croissants and coffee? That must be it, I think. She'll return with a bag of croissants.

I pull on my T-shirt and blue jeans. I set a chair by the bedroom window and sit down, looking out at Venice, hidden behind a curtain partly pulled back. I decide to sit and wait for her. If I am lucky I will see her walking down the street.

It is a beautiful morning.

And then I see her. She is wearing the magenta coat. And yes, her embroidered pants.

Déjà vu. I recall sitting in my hotel room in Florence and being surprised to see her walking down the street to her hotel. So much has happened since then.

And then I recall the very first time I saw her, in Rome. She was on the down escalator, one step above her brother. I recall her smile, her thick black hair, and her hand resting on her brother's arm. And of course the magenta-colored leather coat. It was the coat that first attracted my attention.

She walks down the narrow sidewalk to the street corner. A woman walking. She pauses at the curb, her left foot slightly ahead of her right. She looks up and down the quiet street. No traffic. It is early and only one other pedestrian is out and about. He walks up to the curb and pauses beside her.

I hope that she looks up, that she sees me above her in the window. I imagine she waves to me. I wave back. We both smile.

And then the man raises his hand in the air. Is he going to wave to me?

He holds something overhead, over Istina. What is it? He plunges it downward against her right shoulder. She screams, crumpling on her right side. Her knee drops to the sidewalk. His arm rises and falls, rises and falls.

I want to jump through the window but that is impossible. The woodwork blocks my body. I yell, "Police! Polizia!" The man looks up. Sees me. Just enough time for Istina to struggle to her feet. She begins to turn. Her feet begin to move. And he grabs her magenta coat. He pulls her down. A hyena on a gazelle.

She is on her back now. Her elbows scrambling on stone. Her feet flailing out at the man.

I run to the bedroom door and down the hallway and down the stairs and through the lobby and out the entrance of the hotel . . .

I run to her side. Her body lies on the concrete, slightly twisted, her magenta coat open in the front, a knife plunged deep into her chest. Her head rests on her thick black-blue hair on the hard stone. Her eyes gaze upward, wide open, as if staring into the eyes of her attacker. But he no longer floats above her. Her mouth is open. He left a deep red slash across her forehead. He slashed her face, too—two, three times. He cut her throat side-to-side. She lays quiet on the sidewalk. Wake up! Ascend! Ascend!

The only thing I can do is cry.

I don't know all the details of what happened next. People arrived. And then the police. And then medical personnel. I was given a sedative.

I surmise that someone went through my wallet before I awoke. Found my emergency contact card. Called my great-aunt. She arrived early morning two days later, several long flights from Hawaii. She is amazing.

I realize now that she has had my back ever since I was a kid, ever since she visited Mom and me in that wretched trailer park. She has been looking after me all these years, quietly in the background, helping whenever she has an opportunity. Just like she helped Uncle Keahi.

Reality is sometimes painful. Istina has biologically expired. Her physical life is over. She no longer exists. There is no ascension into heaven or eternal torment in hell. No rebirth. Death is a biological reality. At least it is currently.

Our species' need for forgiveness is unfathomable, and I am no exception. I failed Istina. I made her a promise and I failed to protect her.

After I confessed to my great-aunt, I asked, "Auntie, how do I forgive myself?"

"Liko," she said, "you are a good person. You are learning to think for yourself, to decide right and wrong for yourself, and you want to take responsibility for your actions, or your failure to act. Those are all good things."

"But how do I forgive myself?"

"I don't have an answer for you. I can share a few things that helped me. Would that be okay?"

"Yes, please do."

"I learn and I move on. I don't ruminate on my guilt like a cow on its cud."

I loved her for that. I gave her a hug. "How can I learn and move on?"

"Put away that software application, at least for a while. What do you call it?"

"Aletheia."

"Put Aletheia away for a few months. You interact way too much with it."

"I'd be lost without her."

"Her?" Auntie gave me a strange look. "Give 'her' to me Liko, and I'll throw 'it' in the canal for you."

"Auntie!"

"Talk, share, interact with real people, Liko. Make new friends."

A week passed. My great-aunt left. I started going to the gym.

Several more weeks passed. The museums, the restaurants, the canals and the alleyways, they all lost my interest. The bars, too. There was no solace anywhere.

After another month's stay in Venice, I decided to cut short my European vacation. I would learn cave diving, instead. Now my goal was to return to the Big Island of Hawaii and scuba dive the lava tubes. It was dangerous. I was still claustrophobic. But I just didn't feel like doing anything else.

Penance? A penance for my guilt? I doubt that would work for me, but I haven't tried it. I believe in the Golden Rule, though. It's in my DNA.

Someday I'll turn Aletheia back on.

ABOUT THE AUTHOR

Greg Olmsted is the author of the celebrated *Strong Current Trilogy*, as well as *Maritauqua Island (We Shall Come Awake)*. He has Master of Science degrees in Environmental Health Science and Public Health, and served more than forty years in public health programs. Greg uses the arts to increase public awareness of environmental and health issues. He enjoys skiing and ballroom dancing. He also practices boxing and Muay Thai. Readers can contact him at GregOlmstedBooks.com.

GREG OLMSTED Recommends

THE STRONG CURRENT TRILOGY

UNDER WATER

When you were young, did you want to run away from home? Start an adventure? Explore the world? Liko does. He lives in a trailer park with his mother just outside Las Vegas. But this summer he escapes to Hawaii to scuba dive with his Uncle Keahi. Read about his adventures as he learns about his Hawaiian heritage.

UNDER GROUND

Explosive vapors escape from an underground storage tank. Keahi investigates, hoping to prevent more casualties. But he runs into corruption at the Hawaii Department of Water, Wind and Sun.

Meanwhile, Liko returns to Hawaii for another summer vacation. He is now a high school senior. He rekindles his crush on Toi who is passionate about scuba diving.

And then Liko drops a bombshell: he wants to scuba dive the dangerous lava tubes at Shark's Cove just north of Waimea Bay.

UNDER THREAT

The GLOBAL OIL ACHILLES, a 30 million gallon mega-oil tanker, collides with a longliner. The tanker's steering fails, she is bleeding crude oil, and she is drifting towards the coast of Oahu. Will Waikiki be seriously impacted? Kauai? The Northwestern Hawaiian Islands?

Under Threat describes the dramatic effect of a catastrophic oil spill when a supertanker breaks its back off the coast of Waikiki after colliding with a longliner fishing vessel. Hawaii has two old petroleum refineries on Oahu.

Sign up to receive Email news about Greg Olmsted's new books, giveaways, and more at GregOlmstedBooks.com. Join today!